# HERE

BY THE SAME AUTHOR

NOVELS

*Between Life and Death*

*Do You Hear Them?*

*"Fools Say"*

*The Golden Fruits*

*Martereau*

*Portrait of a Man Unknown*

*The Planetarium*

*Tropisms*

*The Use of Speech*

*You Don't Love Yourself*

CRITICISM

*The Age of Suspicion*

DRAMA

*Collected Plays*

AUTOBIOGRAPHY

*Childhood*

# HERE

A NOVEL BY *Nathalie Sarraute*

*Translated by* BARBARA WRIGHT

*in consultation with the author*

FOREWORD BY *E. Nicole Meyer*

*George Braziller* NEW YORK

Originally published under the title *Ici*
in 1995 by Éditions Gallimard

First published in the United States of America
in 1997 by George Braziller, Inc.



For information please address the publisher:

George Braziller, Inc.
171 Madison Avenue
New York, New York 10016

Library of Congress Cataloging-in-Publication Data:

Sarraute, Nathalie.
[Ici. English]
Here / Nathalie Sarraute ; translated by Barbara Wright
in consultation with the author.
p. cm.
ISBN 0-8076-1423-8 (hardback)
I. Wright, Barbara, 1935– . II. Title
PQ2637.A78314513 1997
843'.914—dc21 97-920
CIP

DESIGN & COMPOSITION:
Neko Buildings & Rancho Typographique

Printed and bound in the United States of America

FIRST EDITION

# *Foreword*

To read Sarraute it is necessary to position oneself differently. The reader must forego the comfort of conventional plot and character in order to enter into Sarraute's often unstable, vacillating world of words and hidden meanings. It is her unique talent at communicating the here and now *behind* words that ultimately produces the universality of Sarraute's work.

Sarraute goes beyond the "noise" of words—the misunderstandings a glance or intonation may inject into a conversation or the "unexpected clash of two opposite meanings of the same word"—to the silent hiding places beneath them. *Here* reproduces the effort to remember a specific word. All of us have felt the frustration of this struggle. And, as her loyal readers age along with the ninety-six-year-old Sarraute, we appreciate all the more the pleasure of finally filling the gaping holes of memory. In addition, we recognize the many interpretations and misunderstandings caused by the simplest and most banal of phrases. Innocent words provoke danger and impose sanctions in the interior world of *here* that we all share. Even the trivial "Do you like traveling?" incites (over)interpretation and fear on the part of the listener, depending on his environment and attitude. Seeking the concealed hiding places beneath words, listeners hover between distress and silence, as they do in many of Sarraute's literary works.

Born in Russia in 1900, Sarraute has lived most of her life in Paris, with studies there, in Germany, and in England. Trained in law, she came late to writing literature. At the age of thirty-nine, she published *Tropisms*, her first book. The minute movements and reactions to spoken words and thoughts that characterize this work continue throughout her oeuvre, culminating in the masterful *Here*. Sarraute discusses some of her literary influences (Dostoevsky, Flaubert, Kafka et al.) and theories in *The Age of Suspicion*. Her early work is considered integral to the development of the New Novel.

Like Sarraute's previous works, *Here*'s dramatic action stems from an oral style composed of the dialogues, repetitions, metaphors, ellipses, and silences of everyday speech. As the search for the correct word reverberates through her head, Sarraute recalls Pascal and writes: "The eternal silence of those infinite spaces terrifies me." This phrase echoes throughout the tightly constructed work. Open spaces battle with enclosed surfaces both in the form of the text (short chapters that sometimes begin and end with the repetition of the same phrase) and in its images (vast limitless spaces compete with enveloped, covered spheres). Much like fear, *Here*'s textual spaces expand, oscillate, and explode only to contract before flickering back to life again. Continual movement distinguishes this text where words can exert vast power.

The drama is reinforced by the ever-present phonetic play of *Here*. While some of the force of the French text is lost in translation, it is reinstated in other subtle ways in English. The French title, *Ici*, phonetically implies stability in its redundant simplicity, but also movement in its explosive pronouncement and in its repetition on almost every page. The brevity of the three-letter word suggests the form of the ellipsis (the three *points de suspension*), which characterizes Sarraute's writing:

> And now in this perfect immobility, in this silence . . . it seemed there could be no presence here . . . suddenly these words: "What's it called again, that tree . . .
>
> But it's nothing, just a brief intrusion, a threat of destruction that will be dismissed in a second . . . "it's . . . it's . . ." the name is there, ready and waiting, it only has to be called up . . . "It's a . . . it's a . . . let's think, it's a . . ."

In English, the title *Here* contains, nonetheless, the repetitive contradictions and universality of Sarraute's work. Where is "here" but everywhere and nowhere? These words, along with the omnipresent "there," recover some of the loss of phonetic play caused by the disappearance of the word *ici*. In addition, as the above paragraph reveals, the short vowel of *ici* remains, albeit in different words. Moreover, the frequent use of the indefinite pronoun "it" (in French "*il*," "*ça*," and "*ce*") reinforces the vague, indefinite zone beneath words that her work captures. So, while the phonetic resonance of the French title *Ici* permeates every pore of the French text (and provides some lovely transitions between chapters), the English remains true to the nature of the book.

As stated in the passage cited above, there is no presence in silence, for, as Sarraute writes, silence is the name "given to that absence of any words exchanged between two people alone, together." The infinite, profound, eternal—and often internal—silences of the Sarrautian world confront the fearful reader who seeks a reassuring word, that forgotten word. Yet, in this, Sarraute's most recent text, one word stands out and does not reassure. "Death" must be avoided, not pronounced, and yet it infiltrates the fibers of this book. For what is an eternally silent infinite space, if not death?

Death, however, as we all know, cannot be avoided. It is perhaps for this reason that Sarraute continually asks: "What's the use?" In so many ways, she queries, "What's the point" if all is cloaked in banal constructions and convention? Perhaps the search for the elusive word will never end, she suggests. If "here must remain pure of all words," then what can possibly quell "the eternal silence of those infinite spaces"?

*Here* is a fulfilling read, and in Sarraute's last paragraph, the forgotten name, "Arcimboldo," reassuringly returns to fill that void and, in fact, provides the last word of her text. "Everything here is only him," she writes. Limits are delineated. The reassurance of the final word counters the reader's fear of forgetting as well as the infinite space of the blank page that follows it. In no small way, Sarraute addresses the many interior spaces within us as well as the eternal silence of the infinite space that awaits us all.

E. NICOLE MEYER

# HERE

NOTE—CHAPTER I

# "Bonjour Philippine"

IN THE DAYS WHEN FAMILIES OF ALL NATIONS used to play parlor games, one of the most charming was "Bonjour Philippine."

When the nuts and fruit were brought in after a meal, if someone took an almond with twin kernels, he (or she) kept one half and gave the other to a fellow player. In the French version played in the first decades of this century, the recipient had to be a family member of the opposite sex. When the two players next met, the first to hold out his kernel and say "Bonjour Philippine" became the winner of the game and was entitled to a "modest present" from the loser.

Some present-day French people used to play this game at their grandmothers' houses, as did some Scandinavians and Germans. The Littré dictionary tells us that it originated in Germany, where an almond with a double kernel was called a *Philippchen*, and that this word came from *Vielliebchen*, meaning "dearly beloved." This, "by alteration and assimilation," became *Philippine* in French.

(Littré warns us that we shouldn't confuse *philippine* with the *filipi* of the Romans . . . !)

# I

It will come back, it can't have disappeared forever, that's impossible, it's been here for so long . . . it was that frail . . . slightly stooping . . . evanescent . . . silhouette that brought it for the first time, they came here together and it remained more deeply implanted here than its bearer.

There was something unusual about it, something striking, which had made it encrust itself here so firmly, and not budge . . . And now all of a sudden, in the place it had taken, where it was certain to be found, there is that yawning gap, that hole . . . "My memory is full of holes," people say casually, nonchalantly, not wishing to dwell on the matter . . . If it isn't indispensable, what's the use of tiring oneself, driving oneself crazy in the effort to fill in that hole, why waste one's time? But what it has left behind it here, this opening, this disjointed, dislocated breach, makes everything reel, the hole must absolutely be filled in, it must at all costs come back, embed itself here once again, take its full place . . .

But nothing remains of it, nothing to hang it on to, to dig it out with, not the slightest special peculiarity, not the vaguest description. Even searching through, and why not, all the first names in the calendar wouldn't help to bring it back to mind . . .

And yet it can't be far away, it's certainly very close, it could turn up at any moment . . . It's probably better not to get so worked up, to be patient, to hope, with all the antennae here mobilized, concentrated, kept in a constant state of alert.

What's that? It's a sort of slight whistling sound . . . barely perceptible . . . it's a little hiss . . . Ff . . . Ff . . . coming from it . . . that's certainly the sound it made . . . Ff . . . but this particular sound didn't come from Ff . . . it came from . . . no possible doubt about it . . . it came from Ph . . . Ph appears very clearly . . . Ph will bring with it . . . Ph is bringing behind it . . . Phi . . . and now Phil . . . Phil is here and the rest will come . . . the rest is coming . . . it's beginning to emerge . . . Phillis . . . but *lis* is too short, too light . . . it's something longer, something rather heavy . . . What! Philomena? . . . What mischievous little devils have amused themselves by sticking those grotesque syllables on to it? They must get off . . . What comes up to replace . . . Proserpina? . . . Proserpina? . . . yes, there, in Proserpina, there is . . . Then Phil must disappear . . . Phil was only an illusion . . . No, though, it wasn't, it couldn't be Proser . . . Proserpina has muddled it all up . . . Phil is here again, Phil imposes itself . . . Phil remains . . . Phil . . . suspended in the void . . . And now . . . prancing around in this vacancy, this disorder, here come Philately . . . Philharmonia . . . Philadelphia . . .

This is the moment when a look in that direction must be avoided, when the gap must be ignored . . . Bring back into the foreground, fill it completely, these wet pavements, this road, these people . . . that man with his walking stick, he shouldn't have stepped down, he should have waited, no though, he is crossing the road, and the lights have just changed to green, he's half hobbling, half running, although he doesn't need to be in such a hurry, the cars are still stationary . . . it's like a distant refrain . . . it's a song . . . it's a dictum . . . it's the words spoken during a ceremony, a rite . . . ritual words . . . and then it brushes everything here aside, it pervades everything, those other fingers, the movement they make to grasp, to extract from the broken shell with its jagged edges . . . to separate . . . they are side by side, covered with rough brown finely veined skin, and to hold out this detached part to those other fingers which in their turn are held out, which take it . . . and then, proclaiming, announcing victory . . . here comes "Bonjour Philippine."

Philippine . . . Philippine . . . again and again Phi-lippine . . . its delightful exhalations spread certainty, reassurance . . . everything around is stable, nicely enclosed, nice and smooth, perfectly sealed, not the slightest interstice through which anything could filter in here, could seep in and cause wavering, trembling . . .

# 2

IT'S THERE AGAIN, IT FILLS EVERYTHING . . . IT stands there immobile, immutable, nothing changes from one time to the next . . . the bit of wall in the blazing sunlight, the big round cobblestones, the greenish-gray grass between them, the massive patinated stone of the old bench, the branches above it covered in pink flowers rising up from the slender, gnarled trunk in fluffy clusters . . . And now in this perfect immobility, in this silence . . . it seemed there could be no presence here . . . suddenly these words: "What's it called again, that tree?" . . .

But it's nothing, just a brief intrusion, a threat of destruction that will be dismissed in a second. "It's . . . it's . . ." the name is there, ready and waiting, it only has to be called up . . . "It's a . . . it's a . . . let's think, it's a . . ." but the talisman won't come . . . usually all you need to do is grab it and hold it out . . . the talisman that wards off the evil eye isn't there any more . . . but what's happening? but this has never happened before, this is the first time . . .

The indifferent, insensitive inspector is waiting on the threshold . . . he will have to be patient, he'll get his proof of identity in the end . . . it was always here, yes, how can it have got lost? we must look everywhere, it's sure to turn up . . .

The bit of wall, the cobblestones, the grass, the bench, have become a little unreal, insubstantial . . . just a decor to make the tree stand out. An anonymous tree, a foreign tree . . . it absolutely has to reveal its identity, it mustn't be released, it must be questioned again and again, kept there, exposed, with its slender gnarled trunk, its branches covered in clusters of flowers that rise up like feathers, like plumes . . . it must be surrounded, pressed, interrogated . . . but nothing emerges, not the slightest indication, nothing that might help its name to resurface . . .

Perhaps if it were treated more gently, taken back and replaced in its real decor where it would flourish without constraint . . . in front of that little whitewashed wall, behind that bench, in that round space between the cobbles where it is rooted . . . perhaps in those familiar surroundings it would let itself go quite naturally . . . but it doesn't give anything away . . . it rises at a distance . . . nothing more than a tree . . . just a tree . . .

Well then, let's make everything round it disappear, so that nothing remains here that doesn't belong to it, they alone, they must be examined very closely, they alone distinguish it from all the other trees, they are its special peculiarities . . . those branches of pale pink flowers . . . fluffy, vaporous . . . they float all around it . . . they surround it with a slight haze . . . Something is becoming condensed, is going to seep out . . . what is it? It's something merry, yes, laughing, it laughs . . . frisky, it frisks . . . frisk . . . Tamarisk . . . no possible doubt, it's a tamarisk . . . at one stroke it's all come back . . . a tamarisk . . . Talisman came quite close, but it wasn't any use . . . how could that coarse, cumbersome *lisman* stuck on to *Ta* have helped to track down, to arrive at tamarisk? Ta-ma-risk.

There's no more hurry . . . we are entitled to linger here, to savor with complete peace of mind . . . The little sunlit square, which had captured and conserved everything in existence that is most intense, most alive, had for a moment been devastated by the exhaustive excavations of avid, impatient treasure hunters, but now it has once again become what it always was . . . Not altogether, though . . . it is inviolable, has been preserved forever . . . the benevolence of Heaven descends upon it . . . it streams from the little bluish-white wall, from the silken reflections of the cobbles, from the grass between them, of a green unlike any other, and from the tree, from the curve of its trunk, from the vaporous clusters of its pink flowers . . . And then comes the moment when those words burst in . . . "What's it called again, that tree?" A harmless intrusion, quickly dismissed . . . the slight excitement of a threat that will immediately be thrust aside: "It's a tamarisk."

Tamarisk . . . by the grace of Heaven . . . Its grace . . . Its benediction . . .

Let it flow slowly, gently fill each of its syllables . . . Ta . . . ma . . . risk . . . Ta . . . ma . . . risk . . .

# 3

And yet it would be enough to telephone . . . "I'm sorry, I'm disturbing you, it's idiotic, I don't know what's the matter with me, I just can't remember the name of that Italian Renaissance painter, you know the one I mean, he painted characters made of vegetables, fruit" . . . immediately the emergency services would arrive, the hole would be filled, everything would return to its place . . . But where would be the satisfaction, the jubilation . . . the proof that the forces that keep watch here are still capable on their own, without outside help, of managing to close what, no matter where, at no matter what moment, may open and allow those vapors to come in and spread themselves here . . . the exhalation, the breath of the irreparable absence, of extinction . . .

Not yet, though, there may still be a chance . . . they never came here one without the other, the moment the image appeared, however indistinctly, the name was there, and the name also conjured up the image . . . each of its syllables was embedded in the head of hair as bunches of grapes, vine leaves, cherries, strawberries, as the zucchini emerging between the two apples of the cheeks, in the mouth, an open pomegranate . . . there was also the same liberty in the name, the same affirmative force, the same boldness . . . bold, yes, bold . . . but bold isn't Italian . . . Boldo . . . Boldovinetti . . . no no, it isn't that, not that at all, that isn't it . . . and that letter tucked away in it, right in the middle, where no one would expect to find it . . . just like that walnut at the bottom of the cheek, like that blackberry . . . Above the head, behind it, something is fluttering in the fog . . . a whitish vault . . . it looks like an arch . . . it disappears, it doesn't belong here . . . Boldo, Boldi . . .

It would be better to give up, to call for help . . . when for once that is so easy, so sure to be immediately satisfied . . . careful, though, not too much haste, impatience, that would be dangerous, there might be sanctions later . . . a reputation as a maniac, a crackpot . . . "He phones me, I was very busy, and he asks me point-blank . . . he seemed anxious, he must have had a sleepless night . . ." Mustn't allow any glimpse of this disarray, this lack of control which means that anything, no matter what, that would have been rejected anywhere else, is welcome to come and establish itself here, to occupy the whole space . . . it must be shown that it was invited here legitimately, in possession of an official pass "in due form" . . . After a moment's conversation, after the customary questions and answers, throw in . . . "I saw, I don't know where, that there's a new album of superb reproductions of that painter . . . his characters were composed of flowers, of fruit . . . I was thinking of ordering it but all of a sudden his name escaped me . . . impossible to remember it . . ." But this time there was no need to take precautions, the sedative injection was administered in an unusually gentle way . . . "Ah yes, it's annoying . . . when that happens to me these days, I don't exhaust myself trying to find it, I've noticed that all you have to do is kick off, and later . . . it's mysterious . . . it's as if a mechanism had been triggered, researches are carried out without our knowledge, and all of a sudden it comes back when we were least thinking about it . . ."

After the thanks, after a few brief formalities, it is possible to have it all to oneself, to contemplate it . . . Arcimboldo . . . so it was he . . . and it was he who made them flutter in the fog, that arch . . . and that absurd, unexpected M . . . it was tucked away in that blackberry hanging from the bottom of the cheek . . . and not bold, of course, but boldo . . . Arcimboldo.

It has found its place again. It is solidly established there. It will never move.

◈ ◈

Just a brief glance to check, no, not to check, there's no point . . . it's just to see the name again for a moment, it's so attractive, so amusing . . . But what has happened? it has vanished . . . the image returns obediently, but the name has deserted it . . . it is no longer embedded in it anywhere . . . the grapes, the strawberries, the apples, the corncobs are there all right, but the name has gone . . .

Arcimboldo! it's a cry, a shriek, the audience are going to sit up, the usherettes are going to come running, the lights are going to come up, they're going to call the policemen on duty . . . but no, nobody moves, all eyes remain fixed on the screen . . . no sound can have been heard outside, it's here that Arcimboldo reverberated with such force, whereas it was a long time since it had been expected, even the void it left behind it had disappeared . . . it's typical of it to choose this moment . . . it's its insolent, provocative, diabolic side . . . just when the postilion has been hit . . . he falls off his seat, all is lost, the stagecoach is going to stop, oh no, luckily someone else takes over, but the Indians are closing in . . . Arcimboldo . . . it has come back, it's here again, that's good, very good, but it's not possible to bother about it now . . . a passenger collapses, a poisoned arrow in his chest, the horses are ready to drop, any minute now they're going to be overtaken . . . there's no place for it here, it has to be relegated to some remote corner . . . neither seen nor heard . . . but it is still there . . . something in its presence there glows, gently vacillates . . . a secret promise, an assurance . . . the assurance that it won't be able to disappear again, that nothing will ever be able to disappear.

# 4

"How is everything?" "Fine, thank you". . . the space here that immediately opens before them, dilates, is about to expand and take on whatever dimensions they give it . . . they can feel quite at home . . . If by any chance they might have been a little apprehensive when they arrived here, they needn't worry, they have nothing to fear . . . they could inspect, sniff at, smell everything . . . the air is pure, it's conditioned, nothing musty, no offensive odors . . . no possible incursions of anything that might be lurking outside, ever ready to sneak in . . . which, suddenly wrapped in a word, in a silence, could insinuate itself here, inconvenience them, frighten them . . . There is nothing here that is hidden, hastily shut away before they enter, waiting for them to leave . . . always on the point of showing itself . . . they can prick up their ears, they won't detect anything, no suspicious movement, no surreptitious shifting . . . Nothing else here but what they had a right to find . . . presentable objects, made, like those they have at home, of solid, tried and tested materials, whose function they have known for a long time, they can use them if they feel like it . . . But in the meantime a space must be cleared so that they can put down the things they have brought with them anywhere they like . . . But perhaps this time they will prefer to see what has been chosen to be presented to them here . . . No, they want to be the first, they even seem impatient to offer it . . . "It's really superb, a lovely surprise . . . How could we have imagined that a tower of those dimensions and that shape and in that place . . . we had been afraid . . . well, not only does it not shock, it doesn't jar with anything . . . quite the contrary . . ."

So it was the tower they had chosen, the tower that, here, had been dismissed as an object fit only for the scrap heap, which should only appear as rarely and fugitively as possible, either when there was no way of avoiding it, or when it could serve as an example of one of those surprising, irreparable errors . . . a real disaster . . .

Conjured up by them, it emerges, it advances, it places itself in the center . . . now it's the only thing here . . . Nothing must make them suspect the low esteem it had been held in, the degradation and ill-treatment it had suffered here, that tower which, where they come from, was honored, which they brought with them to make its powers even greater, to enable it to distribute its benefactions even more widely, even more generously . . . "Whatever side you look at it from, it holds its own, doesn't it?" "Yes, yes . . ." There is no danger for it here . . . Not the shadow of a menace . . . the laws of hospitality, so respected here, protect it . . .

Whatever happens, no confrontations, no conflict . . . It would be intolerable to watch their dismay, their disarray, when they discovered where they had ventured, into what foreign, unknown, hostile country they had brought it . . . we mustn't run the risk of seeing them, incapable of defending themselves, beat a piteous retreat, taking it away with them damaged, defiled.

Without the slightest apprehension, in all innocence, in all confidence, they present it . . . they find words to make clearly perceptible, to make evident its "perfect proportions," its "great simplicity," "the admirably chosen place it occupies, where it harmonizes perfectly with the city, with all the colors of the sky . . ."

But all those ornaments, all those gems they cover it with, which don't suit it, which were not meant for things of its sort, increase the intensity of the feeling of repulsion, of revolt, of impotent fury it provokes, produced by . . . what, exactly? No words have ever yet attempted to capture it, to demonstrate it . . .

Their words are now bringing up to the surface here words of the same sort, of the same force, ones which could hurl themselves on *their* words, snatch them away from the tower, take their place . . . here they come, building up, crowding in . . . "inaccurate proportions" . . . "a servile, impoverished imitation of what elsewhere is a masterpiece of originality, of force" . . . "the worst possible choice of site . . . where it disfigures, dishonors the whole city, whatever angle you look at it from, whatever the time, whatever the light" . . . the words come, they insist, they want to pounce, to launch an assault . . . but on no account must they come out, nothing must allow any suspicion of their existence . . . above all, the silence holding them back must not last too long, it could become one of those "heavy," "reproachful" silences . . . the dangerous words retreat, hide . . . those that must take their place arrive . . . "Yes, yes, you're right, it's quite true."

"Yes, you're right, yes, it's true" . . . the signature affixed to the bottom of the peace treaty after the surrender . . .

But there has been no surrender. Had they not been welcomed into a friendly country? Was it not necessary that perfect understanding should be preserved at all costs? Were they not meant to feel at home here?

And now that they've gone . . . even their image has faded . . . what they have left behind them is still theirs . . . They are still at home here. They are at home everywhere . . . Everywhere, their words have complete mastery . . . they alight with perfect liberty . . . there? . . .

yes, even there . . . and they remain fixed there forever, they stick fast . . . "Admirable" . . . "Amazing" . . . "A gem" . . . "A real marvel" . . . Their constant drone produces a kind of drowsiness . . . a kind of numbness . . . a kind of slight suffocation . . . a kind of very slight nausea . . . oh, so slight . . . it's nothing . . . it'll pass . . . it's already passing . . . things will be all right . . . yes, everything is fine.

# 5

"I MUST ADMIT THAT I CAN'T REALLY BELIEVE IT, but what does it matter if it *is* invented, you're such a good storyteller, I love listening to you . . ."

What's this all of a sudden? What's happening? Everything around is reeling, vacillating, cracking, is going to collapse . . . an earth tremor . . . an enormous blast of cyclonic wind . . . It's a blast of bullets . . . they've penetrated . . . where exactly? what places? there must be a lot of them, how to find them?

But everything is already righting itself, getting back to where it was before . . . the hard, solidly imbricated, indestructible parts haven't been shattered, they have gone back to their place. Nothing can dislodge them.

And that person who dared to attack them, he thought he could destroy them . . . It will be easy to overpower him . . . first aid is already at hand . . . help is on its way . . . "It was true. Make no mistake, it was true, true,

true, yes, true from beginning to end. Not the slightest invention. It really did happen. That was precisely why, that was the reason I told it to you, I thought you ought to know."

So there he is, bound hand and foot. He doesn't attempt to wriggle free. He doesn't budge. He doesn't say a word.

But that sort of rough, brutal treatment won't be enough to subdue him. He'll be careful in future, he'll never allow himself to be fooled again . . . he must regret having let himself go like that . . . but he's going to carry on with impunity . . . he's going to keep forever what he received here, he's going to take another look at it when he gets home, he's probably going to show it to other people . . . well-made objects that he can use to entertain, to amuse . . .

It's impossible to allow him to leave, he has to be convinced first . . . he has to be reeducated, but not brutally . . . gently, calmly, patiently . . . "You see, I might have been vexed at being taken for a braggart, a liar" . . . he makes a gesture of protest . . . "Yes, I know, you didn't mean to offend me, on the contrary, you admired . . . Ah, that's it, we're getting there, that's the important thing, you admired my gifts, my imagination . . ." He acquiesces, he seems reassured . . . "Only, the thing is, you said certain words . . . You said, didn't you: 'But what does it matter if it *is* invented?' You did say that? You admit it?" "Yes, I must have said that . . ."

"You did say it, it has been held against you, it could be, at least at first sight, the worst mistake you made . . ."
"That I said: 'What does it matter?' well, I'll say it again about your accusations, you really are too funny . . . I said: 'What does it matter?' . . . well, what *does* it matter, I ask you, that I said that?"

Above all, mustn't be in a hurry . . . all forces have to be mustered to bring out, to show what is all entangled, shapeless, there . . . it moves, it rises . . . how to get hold of it . . . for a second you think you've grasped it but it sinks again . . . ah, here come the words at last, they catch hold of one end of it . . . that's it, they've got it, they're holding it out . . . "You made a mistake, a serious mistake . . . you couldn't tell the difference between what really happened and a work of fiction . . . Wait . . . yes, it *is* serious . . . you couldn't see what separates them . . . the demarcation line . . . Although it isn't difficult to find . . ."

It ought to be there, within reach, prepared, ready for use, the thing that can make this line appear, but it's still only barely visible, very dim . . . Ah, here it is, it's taking shape for a moment . . . "Look . . . on the one hand there was the thing that happened . . . 'a fact,' that's what people call it, and they even add, quite uselessly—'a fact' would suffice—they often add 'true,' 'a true fact' . . . raw material, very hard, solid, foolproof, it came here uninvited, it encrusted itself, it remained, it exists without any word coming and touching it . . .

but for you to be able to grasp it, for this piece of raw material to be able to go home with you, to become encrusted there as it is here, words are necessary . . . Don't get impatient, that's precisely where the difference lies, there, in the words, humble words . . . they are entirely submissive to it, they stick to it, they cover it with a fine, transparent layer, they embrace its contours obediently . . . it is as if they spring quite naturally from it, it secretes them, it only produces them so that they can carry it over to you, bring it to you just as it is, with the least possible deformation . . . Whereas the words that would have brought you something invented . . . a work of fiction . . . well, how is it that you couldn't see the difference? It's something so fragile, malleable, changing . . . it comes, goes, disappears . . . there should have been words there to welcome it, to shelter it . . . they should have got together and become echo chambers, retorts, alembics, where it could circulate, become amplified, develop . . . words which it would have pervaded, they are full of it, yes, full to bursting, and they would have burst, and then what would have come streaming out of them, what would have flowed in the inflections of the voice, of the tone . . . but what's the use, if you don't feel it . . . although it's surprising that you could have mistaken it . . . you took those meek, self-effacing words, so flimsy and transparent, for words that can make a work of fiction, a product of the imagination, exist and flourish within you . . . truly an attractive product, swathed in those words . . . that was what pleased you, that was what you liked to hear . . ."

Probably a bit numb with boredom, he suddenly sits up . . . "But what on earth are you getting at? I perfectly perceived those words just as you describe them, self-effacing, transparent . . . meek words, as you say . . . entirely at the service of a fact, but those facts were not actually 'real facts,' those facts were only real facts in appearance . . ." "Ah, but that's the point, that's the true count of indictment, you took those facts for imitations . . . for copies . . . you weren't going to let yourself be fooled . . . It was amusing, wasn't it, perfectly well imitated . . . no one would ever believe . . . but you, of course, you are not one of those naive, foolish people . . . you have never made yourself ridiculous by going up and looking more closely at them, those trompe l'oeils, by touching them, trying to discover what they might well disclose . . . you knew they were nothing but painted surfaces . . . Those coins you were given, you didn't even need to test them with your teeth, you knew they were counterfeit, but so skillfully made, so meticulously engraved, gilded, patinated . . ." "But what is all this . . . these counterfeit coins, these imitations . . . I couldn't see trompe l'oeil in what my eye had never seen, in what didn't resemble . . . which was . . ." "Which was, that's it, isn't it, it was implausible. That was why you didn't believe it. But do you have to be reminded that the thing about what is true, what is plausible, is that it may seem not to be true, and that this has happened to it so often and for so long . . . we get lost in the mists of time . . . that a law has been decreed to defend it every time it is threatened by people who find themselves in your situation: 'What is true may be implausible.'"

He seems to be getting impatient . . . "But of course, I know that, what are you trying to tell me? You put words into my mouth that I didn't say . . . I didn't say it was implausible in itself . . ." "Well then, why? What was it?" He seems to be searching . . . he hesitates . . . "Oh, I don't know . . ."

He must be right, he hadn't seen anything of that sort of implausibility that cannot be produced here below, which, for anyone to believe in it, needs a great many concordant testimonies, irrefutable proofs . . . it was not what he had seen, it couldn't be so extraordinary, so amazing . . . Ah, if only it had been possible to bring back even a trace of it, just a sample . . . but how? . . .

It must have been something that was influenced by his presence . . . something that radiated a kind of warmth, gentleness . . . his presence was at times responsible for stirring up, bringing out, propelling toward him, irresistibly offering him something that wouldn't have been seen without him, words that wouldn't have wrapped themselves round it so as to carry it over to him and implant it . . . so that it could remain the same with him as it was here . . . above all no changes, no embellishments, not the slightest fantasy, above all not that.

And anyway, if it had been possible to find it and recall it as many times as one wished, not a single detail would have changed from one time to the next . . . it was intangible, indestructible . . .

And it had been offered to him generously . . . No, not only from generosity, not from a need to give, to share . . . If he had agreed to take it home with him, it might have become heavier, denser . . . Being covered in words, tightly wrapped in them, it would have become even more stable and reliable, more resistant, more durable.

But he had refused to take it home with him and welcome it and keep it as he welcomes and keeps a "true fact." He had refused to grant it the same status, to issue it with a residence permit on that basis. It was only on this condition, by making sure that he didn't accept it as a "true fact," that he could prevent himself from feeling it as a suspicious element, perturbing, upsetting, a little worrying . . . and allow it, on the contrary, to serve him as a pleasant, inoffensive amusement.

If he hadn't been able to grant it the status of a "true fact," it wasn't because he found it implausible, no, he himself said that it wasn't . . . but because it didn't resemble . . . it didn't resemble anything that he had ever perceived here, anything that he had foreseen, conjectured, supposed, guessed at . . . anything that he could have thought admissible here. A "fact" which elsewhere, no matter where, could have been a "true fact," was here only a "displaced fact." It was only as a "displaced fact" . . . obviously with the lack of guarantee, with the insecurity and instability inherent in that status, that he had consented to admit it . . .

He knew when he came in here, and even before he came in, what sort of ground he was entering, he had already inspected the site, he had sized it up, he knew it inside out, he knew what it was possible to find here. Surely not that . . . what had been presented to him . . . Not that kind of thing . . . No, not that. Impossible. He won't accept it.

What arrives here, at no matter what moment, coming from fathomless spaces, and lodges itself, encrusts itself here, enlarges and pushes back even farther these infinitely extensible limits . . . no one can ever know how far they could extend . . . what should have become an integral part of him, a solid, indestructible part of what surrounds him too, which seemed capable of enlargement, of extending its limits farther and farther, wasn't able to penetrate there . . . it was as if it came up against another substance . . . a strange, unknown substance, impenetrable by things that seem to be able to circulate freely everywhere else.

It has its place here, it occupies the entire center here . . . an enormous, smooth dazzling sphere, completely covered in thick glass, mirrors, metal.

Everything that goes out from here is reflected . . . unrecognizable, elusive . . . in its gleaming surfaces.

# 6

"Have you read it?" The words are just about to come spurting out, vibrant with excitement, with enthusiasm . . . forced out by what is there, which is compelled to emerge, to show itself to the person who has come here, who is probably delighting in the anticipation of what he is going to find, of what he is going to be offered . . . who else could so well appreciate it? . . . "Have you read it? . . ."

Just another moment, let them shelter a bit longer in the tranquillity, the security of silence . . . But why hold them back? Haven't they already undergone the most meticulous, the most rigorous checks possible, and there is nothing to stop these words entering the other person's territory, nothing in him which, when they reach him, would be aroused, sit up, try to measure itself, to confront . . . and then fall back pathetically, shattered . . . Nothing over there which, at the appearance of these words, would start crawling humbly, ashamedly, toward obscurity, toward inexistence . . . no, nothing can happen to produce any such painful, degrading sight . . . "Have you read it?" may enter in all security . . . The person who is going to receive these words has never written a book.

Well then, let "Have you read it?" come rushing out . . . the vanguard . . . other words which are not yet formulated will follow, irresistibly driven . . . such as: "Ah, what a book! haven't read anything like it for ages . . ."

Careful, though . . . what's that over there, very far away . . . barely discernible . . . is it really there . . . it's so tiny, so deeply buried . . . it looks as if, under the shock of "Have you read it?", something is beginning to stir a little . . . what can it be? . . . here it comes, it's brushing against, it's detaching itself from . . . it's so old, so eroded, quite threadbare . . . it was deposited here in the past . . . "I would like to write." That's what he had said. "What I want to do later on, is write . . ." and then that was obscured by what he did do later on, at the cost of enormous effort and even with passion . . . it was overshadowed, forgotten . . . he would be the first to be surprised . . . But would he really be surprised? Hasn't there remained in him . . . that may well be where he gets his occasional look of being too modest, almost melancholic, almost nostalgic . . . an unsatisfied desire has remained there . . . and we know, don't we

. . . wasn't it William Blake who felt it, and who said: "He who desires but acts not, breeds pestilence"?

"Have you read it?" wouldn't that make him emit...? "pestilence" is too strong . . . wouldn't one feel something rank, something rather repugnant, emanating from him . . .? it would be disseminated everywhere, all the air here would be polluted . . . even people who don't possess a very keen sense of smell would pick up that odor . . . that whiff suddenly coming from someone . . . just once . . . and it will forever remain the revelation, the proof that he is suffering from a malformation, a secret infirmity . . . it will be the indelible sign of a tainted, weak, petty-minded "nature," insidiously stirred by shameful little movements . . . which are well known . . . classified, they have names: Jealousy. Envy. And what usually, what necessarily goes with them: Malevolence.

Isn't it astonishing?—everyone's extreme severity, people's tremendous exigency, their constant preoccupation with seeing that the rules of the most intransigent morality are strictly, meticulously applied.

If "Have you read it?" were to reveal in his gaze, in a movement of his lips or even in nothing visible . . . just an oscillation in him . . . however brief . . . a clue indissolubly linked to him, his sign . . . Better not to run, and make him run, such a risk . . . Above all, "Have you read it?" mustn't show itself.

◈ ◈ ◈

But there are curious, excited, impatient little imps here, pushing out the words: "Have you read it? . . ." will we, won't we see it appear, that slight vacillation?

But something else suddenly arrives and prevents these reckless, perverse games . . . "Have you read it?" retreats, driven back . . . what these words are going to provoke there, what is going to rise up before them, is "I want to be a writer" . . .

But that's nothing, that's just harmless, one of those children's remarks like "I want to be the Pope," "I want to be a pastrycook" . . . No, the danger must neither be disguised nor ignored . . . "I want to be a writer" . . . we can see him clearly uttering these words, and he certainly looks like an adult.

"I want to be a writer" . . . and nothing else exists here, nothing exists anywhere except this completely enclosed space, surrounded by rigid, smooth walls made of some dark material . . . on all sides, along the walls, iron ladders reach up to the highest landing, at the top, right up at the top under the covered vault where everyone who is a writer is installed . . . All the time, trembling figures are climbing, clinging onto the rungs, hoisting themselves up, falling back . . . down below there is an enormous, swarming mass . . . some of them, precipitated from the supreme heights, are lying there dismembered, others pick themselves up and start again, start climbing again, struggling as if their life . . . what for them is their whole life . . . depended on it . . .

"Have you read it? It's admirable" . . . and we would see, rapidly ascending and then sitting in state there, in the place he had contemplated with raised head, to which he would have given everything to accede . . . a writer. A great writer, of course. No one can be "a writer" without being "a great writer."

It was a nightmare . . . in an instant, just like a nightmare, everything fades . . . "Have you read it?" hadn't budged. "I want to be a writer" had arrived in time to stop it from showing itself.

But neither had there been any "I want to be a writer" . . . it was only an illusion, the result of overanxiety.

What there *had* been, perhaps, but there's nothing so specially terrifying about that, it can be examined with complete peace of mind, was "I would like" . . . "I would like to write" . . . That was more what he said . . . And there, slightly to one side, barely discernible . . . the odd feature . . . the evocation of someone, of a mutual friend, whom he had observed particularly closely, and what he had perceived . . . he was trying to find the words to capture it, to reveal it, and people had passed words on to him, all the words to capture it, to reveal it, and people had passed words on to him, all the words at their disposal, but he didn't want any of them, no, that wasn't it, it was other words he needed . . . collections of words long sought, patiently, prudently chosen, which could perhaps bring to light, make visible . . . "Ah, I would like to write" . . . that was when he said it . . . to write just so as to be able to show what is there . . . that was what he meant . . . "Ah, I would like to write" . . . with a little regret, disappointment in his voice, only transient, though, he was quite content to accept that he had neither the ability nor the leisure . . . there was nothing to make anyone think he would have liked to devote too much of his time and energy to capturing that sort of thing . . .

"Have you read it?" . . . and even before this could be followed by other words that couldn't wait to be released, something in his look, in his face, holds them back . . . his head nods . . . "Oh yes, *have* I read it . . . and there are even some passages . . . I've learned some of them by heart . . . this one, for instance . . ." Words arrive, he pushes them out . . . but does he need to push them? they advance of their own accord, his voice, his intonation, merely help them out respectfully . . . a whole chain of words that extends, nothing can stop it, all that is left here is an open space in which this chain swings freely . . . all of a sudden it stops, it hollows out for itself a little hollow . . . a kind of shelter, a nest, a hiding place for whatever it is that brings welling up, flowing over everything, with him also . . . but there is no longer any "with him," or any "also" . . . all there is now is that little hollow spilling out, overflowing with a delicate, soothing, reassuring gaiety . . .

# 7

We must get hold of one, that one, and force her to look . . . "No, don't turn your head away . . . have the courage to see what is true . . . the truth . . . don't be afraid, it'll be nothing, just an inoffensive little truth, not one of those enormous ones which 'aren't fit to be told,' not one of those that can kill . . . no, not in the least . . . what are you thinking of? . . . it isn't a bandit's lair, here, no one is going to strip you of all your possessions, of all those belongings of yours, which you're used to living among . . . of all that perfection, that great luxury . . . no, it's just this, just a little detail, that defect he has, among so many eminent qualities . . ."

No, though, it isn't possible to get through to her . . . She would search . . . where did it come from? she would go up to it, she would inspect it . . . there's something hidden in the background here, pockets of impurities, a discharge . . . there's a foul smell emanating from it . . . Her face screwed up in disgust . . . Better for her to see nothing, better to let it go by.

◈ ◈

And now, taking advantage of a moment when the space here is void, vacant, she reappears, more present than when she was here in flesh and blood . . . she makes them even more importunate—that impulse, that urge to attack what she brought here, those accompanying troops of hers, carrying her standards, her arms . . . the emblems of Goodness. Of Purity. She gets her companions to parade here . . . they parade, swathed in their splendid uniforms, in their bulletproof vests made of the best-quality materials, goodness, benevolence, love of one's neighbor, humility . . . Who am I to judge?

One after the other she brings them out to be admired . . . This one . . . "Oh no, not that one, that one is well known here, and has been for a long time . . . it isn't possible to say that he is good, he isn't what can be called generous . . ." She raises her eyebrows, she opens her eyes wide . . . the guardians of the Good, always on the qui vive, rush up, drag outside what had been hiding behind the closed shutters and which had just gone on to the attack . . . This is what it was . . . it was mean-mindedness, baseness, malevolence, it was Evil.

The shutters closed? That would be too good to be true. The shutters were not closed, oh no, not here, that might have aroused suspicion. On the contrary, one had to stand at the window, to go out onto the balcony, to bow . . . "Yes, how nice it is that he's generous, that he's good, and that, there . . . and there . . . all around you, there is nothing impure, nothing bad, nothing that is not the very image of the Good."

It has remained imprisoned for too long, been kept secret, and now it's knocking very loudly, it absolutely has to be released . . . She'll stop, she'll look . . . "But don't be so frightened, it isn't what you think, don't call it 'evil' . . . It was you who were spreading Evil, without realizing it, of course, but it will be rectified, you'll see, it will be replaced by what is called Justice, Truth, fine, very respectable names . . . the truth is that he is not generous, the truth is that he refused to lend a small sum of money to someone in need . . ." Her nostrils twitch as if she had got wind of a disgusting smell, her limpid, motionless eyes have a vacant look . . . everything in her closes up, the words won't be able to penetrate her. But no word has emerged, has reached her . . . She can make her troops parade here as much as she likes, she can come back in her own good time . . . And she must think that this is the right time, for back she comes.

There was no way to restrain it, it came out, a little spurt, a slight whistling sound . . . "It isn't altogether true, no one can say that about him, he isn't so generous . . . come on, look carefully at what has just come out from here, they aren't empty words . . . He is quite the opposite of what can be called 'generous,' he refused, he who is so rich, to lend a small sum of money . . . He searches his pocket endlessly to identify the coins in it, he's afraid of giving too much, the beggar's permanently outstretched hand didn't make him feel uncomfortable . . ." Immediately they come running, they inspect, they search, they open every drawer, they don't allow anything to escape them, and they report . . . here's what was found, some fine samples . . . here are some notes, some statements of his accounts hidden and preserved here . . . some sordid estimates of his income . . . the coins they went and looked for at the bottom of his pocket . . . ah, that lot, they never look the other way, on the contrary, it attracts them, they like to dig deeper, to feed on it, that's where they find their best nourishment, that's the only place where they feel fully alive, in those murky waters, in that mud, that mire . . .

But there was no whistling sound, nothing spurted out from here, or could have infiltrated her, not the slightest scrap of impurity, there is no anfractuosity, no asperity in her onto which it could have attached itself, no little shady nook in which a bit of filth could have deposited itself and remained . . . everything in her is smooth and clean . . . and here, too, everything, like her, is perfectly smooth, of dazzling cleanliness . . . no trace here of anything whatever that might be a bit dirty, a bit louche . . .

Her presence here blotted everything out . . . the moment she entered this space she emptied it, she took it over completely, all for herself . . . Emptied it? Not even that . . . everything disappeared as if there had never been anything here before she came . . . No removal, no expulsions . . . whatever might have been here before just sort of quite naturally vanished . . . it went so far away that sometimes, after she has left here, it takes quite a time for what had been here to come back . . . It must probably sometimes happen . . . how can one know? . . . that it never comes back.

Yes, but, after she had gone, something remained here of what she had left, which is hers, which belongs to her . . . and in her absence, as a result of the conditions here, of this climate, it has deteriorated, it has lost its sheen, its beautiful glowing colors . . .

This time, the moment she comes back, it must at all costs be given back to her, she must take it away, even in its present state, the way it has become here . . . "You know those people whose qualities you praised so highly . . ." she doesn't seem to understand . . . "Don't you remember?" "No . . . whom are you talking about?" she looks surprised, shocked . . . "Well, those people we were talking about last time . . . the thing is, I didn't like to tell you . . . but afterward, when I thought back to them . . . I must confess, you must know . . ." she draws back, she's going to call for help . . . where has she strayed? into a lunatic asylum? . . . what's all this sudden aggression, what are these gesticulations, this excitement . . . about whom? about what? . . . "Ah, you've forgotten . . . You know very well . . . you talked about them at length . . . No, you don't know . . . Well, all those people . . ." "But what people? Why all of a sudden? what reminded you of them? . . ." "Yes, it's ridiculous, it remained with me . . . it haunted me . . . I absolutely must . . . you are so pure, you are so indulgent . . . no, don't be afraid, no one is going to say anything bad about them, nothing that isn't fit for your ears . . . all those people we spoke about . . . forgive me for harking back to the subject, it's just to say that they aren't . . . no . . . that's all . . . you'll allow me . . . they are never . . . they can't be . . . in short, they are . . . they're like everyone else, like you and me . . . a bit . . . yes, just this, and then we'll say no more about it, if you'd rather not . . . they are . . . well, you'll allow this . . . nothing bad, nothing at all bad in these words . . . it may even be, if you like, a good thing . . . they are more complicated than that."

# 8

IT SHOULD HAVE BEEN ATTEMPTED BEFORE, WHILE it was still possible, while there was still a chance of "changing the subject" . . . She hadn't been talking about him for long, and his presence was still radiating the kind of vibrations that so many fine and rare qualities and their just recompense do radiate . . . a sense of well-being, of reassurance, and finally of confidence in life . . .

No, though, even at that moment it wasn't possible, after having profited from him and paid him his due, to show him politely to the door . . . Hadn't there already been, almost as soon as she brought him in, something about him that made it impossible to touch him, to edge him gently, quite naturally, toward the door and allow in . . . no, nothing could come in and take his place, no important event, upheaval, imminent threat, war, revolution . . . there was nothing outside that wouldn't have to be given a wide berth, she had with astonishing rapidity magnified him so much that he occupied all the space here and had become an enormous mass which brings pressure on all sides, pushing, keeping everything motionless, preventing the slightest movement . . .

A mass that grows bigger all the time, plastered over with the words she sticks on it . . . "such a rare success" . . . "such strength of character" . . . "such perseverance" . . . She observes it, fascinated, she hasn't had time, it doesn't even occur to her, that's obvious, to bother about whatever might be happening here, all she wants to do, as she would do anywhere else, no matter where, is bring into existence the things that deserve to be universally acknowledged, the things to which she feels obliged, in all honesty, to do justice . . . "that courage," "that intelligence," the words come tumbling out, drawn toward . . . "he knew how to seize his chance" . . . "he made such a shrewd, fortunate choice of his companions, of his partner: a great love" . . . the enthusiasm filling her spills out in her voice, in her tone, propels her words forcefully, makes them adhere closely . . . A statue . . . is erected . . . but it hasn't the rigidity of stone, of marble . . . what is being built under her words is supple, extensible, it's spreading further all the time, the pressure increases . . . under this powerful, this irresistible momentum the walls all around are cracking, and behind, something is beginning to stir . . . something unknown, that had never been seen here before . . . it comes up with difficulty . . . Ruthlessly, indefatigably, the words "circle of faithful friends" . . . "perfect understanding" . . . "capacity for work" . . . "immense talent" . . . find, grasp, shake, force up . . . And here they come, painfully rising, they hadn't budged for such a long time that they are stiff all over, they drag themselves up, they line up . . . The "Ah!" that escapes them shows that they are indeed there . . . shadows, moribund . . . "Ah!" like an exhalation, an expiration, is their response when their name is called . . . "Ah!" and she immediately finds the name on her list . . . Envy . . . she makes a note of it: Present . . . "Ah, really?" . . . Frustration: Present . . . "Ah yes?" . . . Abasement: Present . . . "Ah!" . . . Wasted life: Present. "Ah!" . . . Bad luck: Present . . . "Ah?" Incapacity/Lack of talent: Present . . . Tragedy of not having known a love like that . . . Well? Absent? How is that possible? "Perfect children, all successful," come on, here it is at last, of course that was here, she senses it, just a faint sigh is enough for her . . . Ah . . . Injustice. Bitterness: Both present. She ticks them on her register. Not one fails to answer the call . . .

The call? Yes, the call, they were indeed called. By her. Her words got them up . . . a bugle that she sounded as loudly and for as long as was necessary . . . They were all asleep, they hadn't properly heard it to start with, they were still in their dreams, they were watching the passing images that had come from a beneficent, reassuring world . . . but very soon . . . it was so insistent, more and more strident . . . they were completely awake, they raised themselves . . . they answered, as she knew she would oblige them to answer . . . They were indeed there, she knew it, she came here to make them wake up, that was why she came, to force them to get up.

But perhaps she hadn't thought of it beforehand . . . at first, what she had brought here was intended to impart well-being . . . and then, in spite of herself, because she sensed that the words she had chosen in all innocence, carried away by her admiration, her enthusiasm, were beginning to awaken here . . . what was it? she explored, she searched . . . it was there, it was trying to hide . . . so she went on insisting more and more forcibly . . . it must finally allow itself to be seen, it must show itself . . .

No, there was nothing here before she came, nothing asleep . . . it wasn't true . . . those wretches, those potential murderers, those failures, those pathetic dwarfs didn't exist here . . . She was the only person who had ever tried, who had ever succeeded . . . But she knew how to sow it and make it grow here . . .

Yes, grow, because this was fertile ground . . . Anywhere else she would have been obliged to give up.

No, on the contrary, anywhere else she wouldn't even

have wanted to try, it would have been much too easy . . . what excited her was precisely to see it grow here . . . to convince herself that here too, even here . . . it's exciting to see those pure, innocent, eternal children, those solitary monks absorbed in their meditations, their devotions . . . to see how they resist . . . how the words she throws at them fall, dissolve in their silence . . . but she mustn't become discouraged, they won't resist for long, it exists in them as it does in everyone, like breath, like the circulation of the blood . . . aha, here's something emerging . . . it only needed a little forcing . . . an "Ah!" and then another "Ah?" and then "Ah yes!" and then "Ah, really!" . . . now she's got them, they can't escape, no question of going back to their shelter, of returning where they came from.

They have surrendered, that's good . . . But not the slightest desire to resist must be allowed to remain in them . . . There is a kind of training that would enable them to manage it, a few supplementary exercises . . .

It's a little difficult, painful at first, you aren't in the habit . . . don't look so disdainful, it's true that it isn't what might be called "very refined," it's rather "vulgar" . . . but you see, you're getting there, you are obliged to raise your head and look . . . you find it a bit humiliating? a bit degrading? . . . no no, you'll get used to it . . . But that's good, very good, higher, higher still, look with admiration, with nostalgia at this display of "the good things of this world," at all the wealth, the castles, titles, prestigious jobs, an entrée into society, receptions . . . and here, now just one more little limbering-up exercise: the order of places at table . . . you never think of it, you haven't thought about it for a long time . . . you never did . . . wasn't that sour grapes? . . . and now just one more little effort . . . imagine where you would be placed in the future . . . Oh, it hurts, doesn't it, you can't bear it any longer . . . Well, there we are, I'll leave you . . . I'll go . . . I've already taken up too much of your time . . . I just wanted to pay you a little visit . . . It's such a pleasure to come and see you . . .

# 9

THAT NAME HAD NEVER BEFORE MADE SUCH an impression here . . . a name that didn't bring to mind any passage in a history book, any image of an old village at the foot of an old castle, of a church with recumbent figures, tombstones, legends portrayed in its very ancient stained-glass windows. . . . A name that had only this particularity: the particle "de" preceded, at a certain distance, its charmingly elegant form . . . And this had never seemed to be of any great interest, no one had seemed to notice it, even the bearer of the name had never appeared to be aware of it . . . And then all of a sudden this name, pronounced after a few others while introductions were being made, as soon as it had penetrated one of the guests, had caused that slight movement in him . . . it was almost invisible on the surface . . . but they had all sensed it without being able to explain how, or by what they had recognized it . . . It was so brief, barely perceptible . . . it was as if a little puff of air, a slight breeze, had carried a whisper of this name and made something in him nod, bow, as a sign of acquiescence, of submission, of allegiance . . . and then straighten up with modest dignity, with grateful, happy pride . . .

And immediately, in the person who had been designated by this name, that surprising transformation. What had emanated from him without his knowledge, had rebounded on him . . . a breath that had recoiled on him, something that had ricocheted on him, an image of himself reflected back to him by a mirror . . .

There was something in him that nobody can change, that no merit can acquire, that no demerit can lose . . . which made him different from everyone else here . . . he couldn't help it, nor could they, that was just the way it was, he now felt it "in all the fibers of his being," he knew what it was: the blood flowing in his veins was "blue blood."

And since then, what emanates from him, what spreads everywhere around him . . . all the ambient air is full of it . . . modifies all the actions, gestures, words of the people enclosed here with him, like the transformation of the movements of everyone who is projected out of the terrestrial atmosphere and lives enclosed in the atmosphere of a spaceship.

Look at them, those people over there, listen to them . . . they are still talking perfectly naturally about this and that just as they were before, as if nothing had happened . . . and yet it's clear that something in them has changed . . . they are now seen to have a quality they hadn't previously shown, a particularity . . . they possess the sort of natural immunity that enables some fortunate factory hands to carry on with their work without being inconvenienced by the emanations from certain chemicals floating in the air . . . they are not in the least affected by what is now emanating from the presence of "blue blood."

But here's one who visibly doesn't possess that immunity . . . he has been contaminated . . . it looks as if he's becoming a little bit agitated . . . he too must feel "in all the fibers of his being," he must now see more clearly, more intensely, the color of his own blood . . . It isn't "blue blood," it's true, but it is blood whose color, as we know, is most in harmony with the color of "blue blood" . . . a beautiful pure, deep color . . . a pleasure to look at . . . he absolutely has to show it . . . but how . . . this isn't the moment . . . how can he introduce into the conversation the words that will reveal it, there's no way to interrupt . . . but the words in him, stirred by the waves spread here by the blue blood, rise up, mount, jostle one another, are going to erupt . . . no, just another instant . . . he must first find . . . ah, here's a point where they could be inserted, a peg to hang them on . . . "That reminds me, in my case, well, I can't help it, it's just the way I think . . . I may perhaps have a down-to-earth kind of mind, the sort of rough-and-ready common sense . . ." And now that these words are coming out, they'll be able to hang on there for a moment, just as long as is necessary . . . "Well yes, you know, as far back as my family goes, there's nothing to be found on either side but peasant blood."

But that other one, what's the matter with him? In this area of turbulence we have entered, he seems to be the one who's feeling the most uncomfortable . . . his voice is changing, he's speaking in a funny sort of outdated accent, where did he get it from? That's what they used to call a "gutter" accent . . . Hasn't he in his turn seen what he hadn't noticed before? hasn't he suddenly seen himself as a figure on an anatomical plate which gives a clear picture of the blood filling his arteries and veins, a blood of a dirty, impure, repulsive color . . . a blood that must weigh on him like an accusation . . . Yes, he won't be able to escape it, an appalling verdict is going to strike him . . . well then, let it strike him at once, very hard, he isn't afraid, quick, why wait, why hesitate . . . his voice becomes more and more high-pitched, his words become sluggish, long drawn out, his syllables drag, sprawl, squirm, there's now something in his intonation . . . But of course, that's it . . . you hear me?

that's the way I am, just what you thought, and even more so . . . do you recognize it? it's the blood that circulates in me, as you know, which makes me like this, you can see it very well, I don't hide it, on the contrary, it's *in* me, I shall be struck whatever I do . . . and I do everything I can not to attenuate it, not to avoid the word that always threatens to strike people whose blood is this color, you can see its color, it makes everyone like me liable to the most terrible sanction . . . you must already have applied it to me . . . I didn't realize it then, but now you certainly will, I shall force you to . . . well yes, go on then, apply it to me, louder still, you hear me? . . . it has a very well known name and no one can describe all it comprehends, all its varieties, its subtleties, the innumerable manifestations that this single word covers and which now . . . you can't help it, can you . . . with this single element . . . but you must admit that it's a pretty important one . . . can anything be more obvious, more convincing? you have no option but to apply it to me in all conscience, that's only right, for sooner or later it would anyway be applied to someone like me in whom this blood circulates . . . the sanction that is called "vulgarity" . . .

Vulgarity, quite so, nothing is more repugnant to her, it's really the last thing she can bear . . . Luckily it's not possible . . . that it could be applied to her . . . no one could say that her blood is a particularly beautiful color, but she doesn't look at it, and who does look at it? What does it matter, if nothing in her reveals it, and if, on the contrary, people see in her what they would see if the blood circulating in her were a glorious blue hue.

It may be the influence of the waves the person who has "blue blood" has begun to send out around him that makes her little finger curve even more than usual, rise even higher, keep a greater distance from the other fingers of her right hand which are delicately holding the handle of her teacup while she purses her lips to take a dainty little sip . . . and that makes it easier to hear the modulations of her voice and the charmingly graceful play of her slight accent, a very slight, delightful English accent, in the very "choice" words she uses, in short, in her whole appearance, her aspect . . . she doesn't do it on purpose, she isn't making the slightest effort . . . it's the sensitivity she is so lucky to possess, her refinement, that makes her look exactly like . . . that makes her just as "distinguished" as she would be if *her* blood, too, were of that glorious blue.

As for him, you wouldn't believe it, and in fact no one does, it's so amazing, the only way one can explain it is that he must have defective eyesight, a kind of color blindness that he doesn't even seem to be aware of, his picture of the color of his blood which is so ugly, murky, painful to see for anyone with normal eyesight, is that it is a more beautiful, intense, pure color than the most beautiful blue blood . . . He has certainly always seen it as being of that color, he doesn't remember ever having seen it otherwise, how could he have, isn't one color-blind from birth?

It's probably this inborn image of the glorious color of his blood that gives him such dignity, such tranquil assurance, such pride . . . it may be this pride that is responsible for his casual, rather nonchalant air . . . one might even detect a touch of disdain in it . . . in short, there's something about his whole person, about his gaze, about all his features, that is usually described as "noble," as "aristocratic."

Perhaps he imagines that the people who see him and know him cannot fail to apply these words to his blood also, that they see his blood as he himself sees it, as being of a color that is at least as "noble" as that of the most beautiful blue blood?

If he only knew how wrong he is! . . . how is it that he doesn't realize that we have taken off, and that in this spaceship in which we are now confined, we are subject to new laws?

Here, even if he deserves to be acknowledged as possessing all the qualities designated by the words "noble," or "aristocratic," there is no outward sign to show that these same words can equally be applied to any other blood than "blue blood." Nothing here can ever for a single instant make anyone forget the color of his blood.

In this new atmosphere, words circulate, hang in the air, ever ready to alight . . . words like "aristocratic" . . . like "vulgarity" . . . it is as if there are currents carrying them toward certain points, away from certain others, according to strange laws, hitherto unknown here . . . If you observe them carefully, you can see that what regularly attracts them, or on the contrary drives them away, is the presence of blue blood.

Whatever the manifestations toward which the word "vulgarity" ought immediately to be attracted and to which it ought to be applied, blue blood prevents this word from sticking to them and even from approaching them . . . on the contrary, the word "aristocratic" is attracted to them and disguises them . . . as well as all accents, gestures, manners, eating habits, ways of dressing, features, the line of the nose, the nostrils, the lips, the ears, the fingers . . . in short, there is no end to the list of things to which blue blood attracts the word "aristocratic," but which, in the absence of blue blood, are pounced on by the word "vulgarity."

The absence of this blue blood, which ensures both efficient protection and the presence of blood of a disagreeable color, exerts a truly prodigious force of attraction on the word "vulgarity" . . . it needs no more than the appearance, at the corner of a lip, of an eye, in a movement of the hand, in the curve of an eyelid . . . whatever . . . it's undefinable . . . but, until something better comes along, the word "vulgarity," ever vigilant, always on the lookout, swoops down on it, and doesn't let go.

All this, this surprising perturbation, because all of a sudden a glance . . . barely a glance . . . had taken in that movement of gratitude, of acquiescence, of allegiance, which made apparent something he was no longer aware of, made it overflow from him, spread waves everywhere here . . . those waves which always do spread the moment it appears . . . the color of blood.

# 10

"Do you like traveling? . . ." And immediately everything here shrinks. It has become a scaled-down space surrounded by notice boards where, on sheets of white glossy paper, color photographs produce . . . What? what is it?

"Do you like traveling? . . ." and a "Yes" emerges . . . a "Yes" equally smooth and shiny, a "Yes" like a great big multicolored egg comes trundling out, stops: "Yes."

Shouldn't this have been enough to ensure that another time, even before something like "Do you like traveling?" arrives, all possible precautionary measures have been taken here . . .

But here, these slight accidents only cause doubts about whether this place can be in good condition, of good quality, when something so trivial . . . "Do you like traveling? . . ." can provoke such changes, justify such suspicion, such caution.

"Do you like traveling? . . ." Stop anyone, ask anyone

"normally constituted," who is not a certified lunatic: "What effect does this question have on you? what would it do to *you*, tell me frankly, if someone asked you: 'Do you like traveling?' . . ." But no one here would ever dare run the risk of letting that vacillation appear in his eyes, of allowing any shadow of anxiety to pass over his face, before the words come . . . "Well, but that's a question you often hear asked. One of the most ordinary, normal questions . . . What's wrong with it?"

And quick, "What effect would it have on you?" has to be stifled, taken back, and what must be sent out is "But of course, you're right, it has no effect on me either. I don't know why I brought it up" . . . and "What effect would it have on you?" must be kept locked away, triple locked, before they come and investigate here and insist on knowing the origin of those strange noises, like muffled moans, groans . . . Why did you cry out? What's the matter then? What's happened then?

No no, it was nothing, there were no cries . . . it was a false alarm . . . Here too "Do you like traveling?" did absolutely nothing, had not the slightest effect . . . Here too "Do you like traveling?" was accepted without any problem.

So "Do you like traveling?" and the effect it produced here, which it would never have produced anywhere else, has been blotted out, forgotten . . . not the slightest notice was taken of it . . . and now, faced with one of those people who ask, or who would ask—why not? what's wrong with it?—this ordinary question anywhere, and who could ask it here as well, oh come on, whatever are you imagining? . . . this inoffensive question: "Do you like traveling? . . ." comes out freely, without the slightest hesitation, as if it had come out into the most favorable climate, the same climate as here, and had been deployed . . . "That gesture he made . . . with that permanently inscrutable face, those frowning brows . . . that movement of his hand which was held out as if grudgingly, which brushed against my cheek, pinched my ear, patted my shoulder, and nothing touched me so much as that movement, as if holding back, preventing the overflow of an excess of tenderness, of approval . . . And that hand digging into his pocket, bringing out some bonbons, some coins, and furtively slipping them into my childish hand" . . .

"Where does he come from? Who is he? Where did you find him?" "Don't you remember?" "No, he doesn't come from here." "What do you mean, not from here? But you gave him to us . . ." "Gave him? . . ." "Of course, you gave us his description . . . it's the best possible robot-portrait to allow everyone to recognize him immediately: The Rough Diamond. There's no way anyone could fail to see him . . . it's him all right, don't tell me that when you were describing him . . ." "I have never described him . . . How could I? He's indescribable . . ." "But that gesture, that hand pinching the cheek, pulling the lobe of the ear . . . exactly the way Napoleon did, incidentally . . . ah, we hadn't even thought of *him* . . . and that generosity . . . so characteristic too . . . well, it's him all right, we're bringing him back to you exactly as you gave him to us, The Rough Diamond . . . don't deny it, you made such a good job of him, he's perfect . . ."

And here they are now, passing, walking by . . . Look at them, you know them so well, they come from your part of the world, that's where they live . . . here are the Tamed Shrew. The Perfect Couple. The Great Genius. The Femme Fatale. The Romantic Poet. The handsome riders dressed in the costume of the last century, impeccably mounting Thoroughbred horses in delightful English engravings . . . "But there's some misunderstanding, there has never been anything like that here . . . that comes from somewhere else, it comes from your world . . . It has never seemed possible that starting from that basis, from that line, from that gesture, from an expression—one among others—which suddenly appeared, surfaced . . . that on that basis you could . . . Ah, but why complain, why become indignant, after having given away, without asking oneself to whom, those little living fragments . . ."

It would have been better to have shown a little restraint, a little reticence, not to have been so outspoken . . . but the charm, the fascination that emanated from them made it tempting to insist, to try to force . . . as if to overcome some sort of resistance, to make them at all costs accept . . . to impose . . . to collect impressions, to accumulate details, to forge ahead, as if in a daze, forgetting, ignoring the danger, and to have gone and flattened oneself over what was inevitably going to rise up there . . . The Rough Diamond. The Femme Fatale. The Romantic Poet. The riders in the English engravings . . .

Yes, that was where, one must be fair, that was where it came from, from their resistance, their opposition . . . they didn't want to have anything to do with all that grace, all that charm, they didn't want it to make them squeeze out any of that sort of dubious, tainted admiration which gives the impression that something is timidly stirring underneath, something like jealousy, envy, resentment . . . so they manufactured and brought here . . . it was what's called a "tit for tat" . . . just look at the people who frequent your place here, just look at whom we have met here . . . That Rough Diamond. That Femme Fatale. That Romantic Poet.

As when after a shock, an accident, you come round and see them bending over you sympathetically, solicitously

. . . You seem stunned. You don't recognize them? But surely that was what you wanted? All we did was obey you, we're fascinated, submissive, we are under the charm, how could we not be? Here they are, just as you must certainly have thought we were going to return them to you . . . That's simply the way it is, we couldn't do anything else . . . You don't like it much, but what can we do about it? . . . It's everyone according to his means, his possibilities, isn't it? . . . You don't want it? But you have to accept it . . . True, it isn't quite the thing for persons of taste, of refinement, but we . . . you should have expected that . . . it's all we are capable of giving you . . . The most beautiful girl in the world can only give what she has.

# 11

"It's funny, you sometimes use expressions . . . certain words . . ." "Really? but it seems to me that I talk like everyone else . . ." "The thing is, one doesn't hear oneself speak . . ." "Yes, that's very true . . . In any case, I had never realized it . . . But actually, what words? what expressions?" "Well, the word 'one,' for example . . . You start by saying 'I,' which is appropriate, you say 'I am going to do this or that,' and then you abandon the 'I' and put 'one' in its place . . . it's rather odd . . ."

They search, they finger . . . everything here was covered with a plain fabric, all of a piece . . . but there they noticed the trace of a break . . . where an "I" should have been, they saw a "one" appear . . . they tap the wall a few times, it doesn't give back the same sound, somewhere, concealed behind it, there must be a cupboard, a hiding place . . . they are intrigued, they would like to see . . .

Yes, that "one" which slips in there . . . No one had ever said they'd noticed it, people are so sensitive, so prudent, they don't want to show, or even to let anyone suspect that they have detected certain signs . . . a tone of voice, an intonation, an accent . . . for that would risk bringing to light the entrance to a secret passage which might lead far, very far, God knows how far it might lead, where it might end . . . how could anyone dare enter it? But this time, let's be fair, this "one" in place of "I" can only reveal the existence behind it of a narrow, closed cubbyhole, of a little drawer which one might allow them to see . . . it could be amusing to open it in front of them . . . "You're right, it *is* rather funny, that 'one' all of a sudden instead of 'I' . . . although it doesn't really surprise me, I probably do say it sometimes . . . but when, actually, apropos of what?" "Well, when you're talking about your efforts, for example . . . You said: that's all 'I' think about, it stops me sleeping, it's as if my whole life depended on it and then when things are really going badly, 'one' finally gives up, and then, after a while, 'one' goes back to it, 'one starts again' . . . It was a question of *you*, of you alone, you could only have been talking about yourself, and all of a sudden that 'one' . . ." "I don't think there's anything so strange about that . . . It probably occurs quite often without anyone noticing . . . In situations where the 'I' may be afraid of putting himself forward too much, of giving himself too much importance . . . When the 'I,' a little embarrassed at revealing so much of himself, at making himself too conspicuous, wants to efface himself and calls upon 'one' to cover up for him, so that he can become anonymous, merge with others like him, become one of them, protected by them . . . isn't everyone the same? 'One gets discouraged and then, of course, one starts again . . .' It's to allow everyone to participate, 'to put them in the picture' . . ." But this accumulation of explanations doesn't really seem to be convincing them . . . "No? you don't agree? . . . and yet it's pretty obvious . . . Maybe it implies a certain modesty . . ." But it seems that "modesty," which after all they are familiar with, doesn't satisfy them, nor does "humility" . . .

They're going to take away this 'one,' analyze it with whatever products they possess, classify it among the other samples they've taken from here . . . an abundant collection . . . what else can they have picked up? "What other things do I say that surprise you?"

They are silent for a moment, they must be consulting their notes, their observations . . . "Well . . . you use the masculine when it should obviously be the feminine . . . When you were talking about a woman, one of your close friends, you told us that you said to her : 'Mais tu es complètement fou!'" "Ah yes! I did say that . . . yes . . . 'Tu es fou' . . . that comes from a custom we had in my family . . . it goes back to my childhood . . . 'Fou' wasn't considered offensive, but 'folle' was . . . This was tacitly accepted by us all, at least I don't remember anyone ever speaking about it . . . There were other words like that which no one could take offense at . . . Like 'salaud' . . . 'Salaud' was only permitted in the masculine, and then, naturally, only when said in a certain tone of voice . . ." They nod, they smile . . . "Yes indeed, 'salaud' in the feminine . . ."

They seem satisfied with so much willingness . . . that of the patient reading the letters on the oculist's test chart and making every effort to give him the most authentic, the most exact answers possible so as to help him not to get his assessment wrong, to arrive at the correct diagnosis.

"Then since you want to know . . ." "Oh yes, this interests me . . ." "You also sometimes say . . . and here you really are the only one . . . You say: I'm going to tell this in the style of . . . you use an English word . . ." "Ah, so I do, I say 'Jingle' . . . 'in Jingle style' . . . I get that from my father . . ." "Was your father English?" "No, but he loved *Pickwick Papers* when he was young . . . he sometimes used to read us bits of it . . . There was a Mr. Jingle in *Pickwick Papers* who always expressed himself in telegraphic style . . . Ah, of course, I should have said 'telegraphic style' . . . but 'Jingle style' has remained with me . . . when you're in a hurry, when you have no time to lose . . . 'Say it in Jingle style' . . . 'I'll tell you in Jingle style' . . . But how could I have, to you . . . How could 'Jingle' have escaped me . . . No wonder it surprised you . . .

and that I didn't notice it . . . That's what comes of not hearing oneself speak . . . But not to hear oneself to such a point . . . I find that a little worrying . . ."

These propositions have fallen into a profound silence and remain immersed there. Not a word of reassurance . . .

And then all of a sudden: "Who is that 'he'? Whom are you talking about? Look, that's another good example . . ." This time their tone is irritated, almost violent . . . So much submission, so much eagerness to retrieve things for them which would otherwise have remained buried . . . not very deeply, it's true, but which even so have been dug up and obediently deposited at their feet . . . this gave them confidence, made them aware of their power . . . They must have decided that it was time to restore a bit of order here, to stop condoning so much sloppiness, so much negligence . . . in the end it becomes . . . it does in fact constitute, a lack of courtesy . . . "Who is that 'he'? Who is that 'he' you were talking about?"

They must know perfectly well whom that 'he' refers to, but they want the rules that are applied everywhere to be respected here too . . . "Who is that 'he'?" "But it's still the person I was telling you about . . ." "But you weren't talking only about that particular person, so how do you expect anyone to guess? You often say 'he' or 'she' or 'they,' as if everyone was supposed to recognize

. . ." "Ah yes, that must be yet another of my quirks . . . It may be due to my bad habit of thinking that you are at home here, in the same element, 'in the same boat' . . . it's ridiculous . . . I don't know why I have that impression, I'm wrong . . . it seems to me that the people I've been talking about . . . that they are just as present in you as they are in me . . . well, I mean what emanates from them . . . that's what counts . . . what's the point of repeating their names . . ." "Ah, so that's why . . . we, on the contrary, some of us have the impression that you are only talking to yourself . . . that you forget, or in any case that you don't bother, to take account of our presence . . . Another thing that has the same effect on us is the way you so often keep skipping from one subject to another . . . one may well be used to it, but one is still sometimes rather shocked . . ." "Ah, my playing leapfrog from one subject to another . . . that's true, I've often been told about that . . . that I have a grasshopper mind . . . And anyway, I sometimes notice it myself . . . it must be very irritating . . . I ought to control myself better . . . but I don't usually notice it until afterward, or until someone points it out to me . . . they often laugh about it . . . But in this case, actually, I don't know, I can't quite see . . ."

It keeps coming all the time from all around . . . an incessant movement . . . the silent procession of souls in torment . . . deprived of the words that alone would enable them to become embodied, to burst in and suddenly break the thread of the conversation which in all legitimacy, in all security, is being conducted in the center here. From time to time, something that is waiting for the right moment to jump in begins to lose patience . . . but there's nothing to be done, it mustn't show itself, it's an irrelevancy, it's malapropos, and anything that is malapropos must remain so.

But now there occurs a slight breach in the chain of propositions . . . it looks as if between its links there could be a place for a kind of solution of continuity in which this particular irrelevancy could well insert itself . . . it can't hold back any longer, it simply has to come out, words present themselves to it, hard, solid, powerful words are going to encase it and allow it to leap out . . . "It's dreadful, I don't know whether you've seen it, no one talks about it, no one decries it strongly enough, what's still going on these days, and on such a scale . . . Yesterday I saw an astounding reportage . . ."

Extremely surprised, they look at what has just been introduced, which really *is* malapropos, it could only have come from what they call a grasshopper mind . . . it should have formed part of a completely different circuit . . . but however malapropos it may be, one can't decently reject it . . . a moment of sad, respectful silence is observed, words from a great distance are brought in to indicate sympathy, commiseration . . . "Yes, it's horrible . . . Unfortunately . . ." And then, with the zealous aid of everyone here, the propositions that form a legitimate part of this circuit follow on . . .

All of a sudden, in that space around the chain of propositions, in which there was a continual coming and going of what, deprived of words, cannot, must not show itself, a wind blew . . . everything rises, flies up . . . there, in that place where it always used to be found, there is a void . . . a patch of nothingness opens up and something escapes through it . . . like the harbinger of the definitive disappearance, of annihilation . . . no though, perhaps not, not yet, words come rushing up to call for help, impossible to stop them, it's only possible for a split second to try to prepare their entrance, to make them look a bit more presentable, a bit more decent . . . "Forgive me, it's ridiculous to talk about it all of a sudden, but it's just come back to me, I don't know why . . ." But the words that were to have followed are intimidated, and haven't the strength to attack, they retreat, they hide . . . for a moment the chain of propositions had started moving again . . . it slowed, it was about to stop . . . but it mustn't . . . other words come rushing up to repair what might have been damaged, to get it going again . . . "No, I don't know what got into me, do forgive me . . . To come back to what we were saying, yes, I agree with you, but even so we need to take into account . . ." But there's nothing to be done . . . once again everything in the background starts seething, a stronger gust lifts up piles of paper, drawers burst open, it'll ease off, the void will be filled again . . . There it is, that long, brown, thick envelope . . . it must be there . . . no, it isn't there, it disappears, it slides into the wastepaper basket, a hand picks up the basket, empties its contents into the dustbin . . . it's been taken away, it's lost for ever . . . impossible to hold back this cry . . . "I've lost, I've just realized, I don't know how I shall ever . . ." And now, through the gap that this call for help has opened, assistance arrives . . . "If you write and explain, you might perhaps get . . . they may have kept a duplicate there . . ." "Ah, you think so? You've known a case . . . Oh, thank you. Oh, do forgive me . . . my grasshopper mind again. . . ."

They are dumbstruck, in both senses of the word . . . they don't understand . . . Where from? How did it get here? How did it manage to get through all the checkpoints? They examine it for a moment . . . "It's delightful, indeed it is, very 'poetic' . . ." But "poetic," even said in that tone of voice, doesn't suffice to indicate their disapproval, their contempt for this violation of the rules, this offhandedness . . . an eccentricity that calls for some clarifications, some justifications . . . "But why all of a sudden now? We were talking about the recent demonstrations . . . about the latest opinion polls . . . What's the connection? What made you think about it?" "It was a recollection of my last trip abroad . . . I don't know how it came into my mind . . . it still comes back and haunts me . . . it was so astonishing, so lovely, those ancient little squares, those houses so incredibly intact, so well preserved . . ." The tone of voice that bears these words must surely be "full of conviction," full of emotion, a dreamy, haunted tone, the words emerge of their own accord, as if from a little light that has just come on over there, as if from a spring that is just welling up . . . But what they manage to evoke seems so banal, so commonplace . . . images of such pathetic insipidity . . . "Well, it's idiotic . . . but I really was following, I didn't miss a word, and you know very well how much it worries me, as it does you, how much importance I attach to it . . . It's funny, don't you think, the impression we sometimes have of being split in two, of functioning on two levels at the same time . . . Don't you think so?" No. Their silence shows it: they don't think so.

It looks as if all these malapropisms which never stop marching up and down in that ambulatory around the conversation, prudently awaiting the right moment, have become more audacious, they take the liberty, whenever they feel like it, of hop-skip-jumping into it, armed with words, of cutting into it no matter where, and this time the conversation has been revolving in the same circuit for far too long for their liking, it's flagging, it's making no headway, it's dragging its feet

. . . so a malapropism jumps forward, takes the plunge, and is followed by other outsiders which, like the real outlaws, the real brigands that they are, steer the procession into a completely different direction.

After a moment's disarray . . . but what's happening? but where are we going? . . . After a little jolt, the conversation gradually gets going again . . . an unknown route which leads to places hitherto . . . It's so futile, it's so vulgar . . . the sort of places of amusement where one would be ashamed to be seen . . . to meet . . . but gradually, what had only been visited in secret, without words that might reveal it, words bring it here where it displays itself in broad daylight, as the most decent, the most honorable, and even the most apposite of remarks, thanks to them the conversation livens up, the excited propositions push, shove, play leapfrog over one another . . . "No no, the most amazing thing is that he wasn't even her lover . . . no one knows how she managed to give up . . . Haven't you read what she declared though? . . ." "It's not possible! . . . she said *that*! . . ." "Yes yes, no doubt about it . . . me too . . . I heard it too . . ."

But that's only an isolated example, even a fairly exceptional one, the sudden assault of these malapropisms doesn't often produce such beneficial results.

"Let the dead arise!" violently, aggressively, this erupted . . . "But whatever are you talking about? What's the connection?" Decidedly, though, these outrageous malapropisms can't contain themselves any longer, they think they're above the law, and this particular one: "Let the dead arise!" . . . just when they were calmly speaking of Dedication . . . the conversation is broken, it stops, then it takes quite another direction and hastens to the rescue of "Dedication," which has been kidnapped, which it wants to deliver . . . "Oh come now, it was 'Dedication' we were talking about, the 'Dedication' of a book . . . D-E-D . . ." But there's nothing to be done, "Dedication" has now been taken prisoner . . . "Let the dead arise! Let the dead arise!" . . . it has been emptied of its meaning and linked to "Dead," which injects it with an unknown, disconcerting, impenetrable meaning . . . which renders it completely unrecognizable . . . but it's hopeless to try to rescue it . . . "It wasn't 'the Dead,' 'the Dead' have nothing to do with it, it was 'Dedication' we were discussing" . . . there's no way to deliver it. We must resign ourselves, it's irretrievable . . . "Dedication," so useful, suitable, respected, surrounded by words of its own kind, a malapropism has caught it on the hop, expropriated it and turned it into another malapropism . . . and *what* a malapropism . . . scandalous, demented!

But what's the use of going on . . . one would never come to the end of the search, one would lose oneself in everything that might happen in the midst of so many hops, skips, and jumps, so many grasshoppers, so many frogs . . .

# 12

SO THAT WAS IT . . . BUT HOW WOULD IT HAVE been possible to discover it, even to suspect it . . . they had to come and admit it themselves . . . but why "admit"? . . . they had nothing to admit, they didn't feel the least bit guilty . . . they were the victims of their extreme sensitivity, their receptivity, their sympathy, which made them react as one person, suffer . . . They had had to let quite a time go by before venturing . . . And anyway, they had wondered what good their presence could do . . .

They hadn't had the effrontery to imagine that they could be strong enough to manage, even for just a few moments, to deflect, to dislodge what, as everyone knew, had entered here in force, occupying everything, reigning over everything . . . what they didn't even dare to call by its name: Tragedy . . .

Nothing, though, could be more worthy of that

name. More pure. More authentic. No possible comparison with those sufferings that sometimes usurp the name of "tragedies" . . . they may indeed be immense, but they are blurred, smudged . . . anyone who is overwhelmed by them prefers not to show them . . . if he were to commit the imprudence of allowing them to be seen, if he were to go so far as to describe them by the noble word of "Tragedy," he would run the risk of spreading around him something impure and blurred like them, of making it flood back on him . . . a defiling, demeaning kind of pity.

This kind of Tragedy, on the contrary, was until quite recently still publicly recognized, it hoisted its colors with pride . . . its black veils and crepes, ties and armbands . . . for a precisely measured length of time it occupied a rank that obliged everyone who approached it to conform to the well-established, reassuring rules of a particular etiquette . . . it was enough to follow them . . .

But now that Tragedy has abandoned its outward signs, now that it has been stripped of its decorations, of its uniform, now that it can go incognito anywhere, at any time, in the most ordinary clothes . . . now that it can live clandestinely, in whatever way it wishes, no one ever knows where it may be hidden . . . in places where one least expected to find it . . . The slightest little thing . . . what thing? how to foresee it? . . . can all of a sudden reveal it . . . a disturbing reflection . . . a shadow

. . . one never feels at ease, one must always be on one's guard . . . one never knows "which way to turn" . . .

But they are mistaken . . . Tragedy has left no traces here that could make them feel the least bit uncomfortable. Their presence here immediately drove it very far away, much farther away than this ambulatory, where everything that is waiting for the right moment before making its entrance is pacing up and down . . . until they have gone, there will never be a right moment for Tragedy.

As soon as they arrive here, everything is wide open to admit anything cleansing, refreshing, vivifying that may come from all parts, no matter where, and to allow it to spread everywhere . . . "Ah, that's worth seeing . . . an astonishing show . . . a marvelous innovation . . . no one had ever dared like that to transform . . . I've never much liked opera, myself, with rare exceptions, but this time I was absolutely delighted . . . and there was so much comedy in it . . ." "Yes yes . . ." They say these words almost automatically, almost as if to get rid of, to sweep away . . . they look preoccupied, it's as if they've seen something coming, taking shape very vaguely . . . but there's no possible doubt, that's what it is, it's approaching . . . Tragedy . . . it's here, it has covered all the distances, got through all the barriers . . .

It was the sudden appearance of the word "Comedy"

that must have attracted it . . . don't people talk about the "attraction of opposites"? Or perhaps we might rather say that "Birds of a feather flock together"? But of course not, what a peculiar idea . . . it was they who called it up, called it back . . . Comedy, welcomed here, installed and made at home here, shamelessly exhibited, showed them how disrespectfully, how cruelly Tragedy had been banished from here, cast down, consigned to oblivion . . . but they intend to release it, bring it back, reinstate it with all its rights . . . Their casual, disdainful "Yes yes" immediately swept away, put an abrupt stop to, all those operas, songs, and dances, all that indecent frivolity which, if they didn't put things to rights, would turn this place into a pleasure palace . . . And, after their dismissive "Yes yes," they produced a silence that allowed Tragedy to be welcomed here with all due respect . . . and here it is . . . it's advancing . . . it's back.

But this name, Tragedy, can no longer manage to encompass everything that is now spreading here, occupying the whole space . . . But how can it be the *whole* space? when it is a space that has no limits . . .

"And I would even say that it's still worse than what they tell us about it . . . what you find there . . . you wouldn't believe it . . ." How could they not do their best to help such courage, such devotion . . . so much effort to build that wall here, ever higher, ever thicker . . . to accumulate all those materials chosen from among the most solid, the most weatherproof . . . brought back from everywhere, no matter where . . . catastrophes, earthquakes, floods, famines, exterminations, wars, scandals, landscapes, journeys, adventures of all kinds, exciting expeditions to discover a hitherto unknown world . . . everything is seized, removed, and brought back to erect that rampart whose purpose is to protect them against what threatens to break in here and inconvenience them . . . and they absolutely must contribute . . . they search, they devote themselves, they are prepared to give everything they happen to have at their disposal to ensure that what is there, in the background . . . they sense it pushing, pressing . . . Tragedy . . . to ensure that it can't infiltrate, demolish . . . no, here are some unassailable materials . . . "I was just about to mention it to you, it's extremely important . . . it upsets all our convictions, all our prejudices . . ." But why make such an effort . . . it's unequal combat, it exhausts everyone . . . they are certain that as soon as they have gone, Tragedy, with a single thrust, will transform all these splendid fortifications into a little heap of rubble.

But this time, here, there is no hint of what frightens them so much, not the tiniest vestige of Tragedy . . . everything that is here, as it would be everywhere else, is turning, reaching toward what has entered here, which was violently flung in from outside and which immediately appropriated the whole space . . . An unknown, somewhat strange object . . . And they have come at the right moment, perhaps they will be able to help to catch it, to keep hold of it, to examine it . . . "Astonishing, isn't it? . . . What have you heard? What do you think about it?" "Yes indeed, it really is very disconcerting . . ."

But how is it possible? Even this time, even at this moment, they have seen it again, they can still see it, they feel its presence all around . . . it's what made something insinuate itself, creep into their response, something like a very slight lack of assurance, like a barely perceptible hesitation . . .

What they were shown, what unfolded before them, appeared to them as if it were a painted curtain hung over it to screen it, but they are not mistaken, it's there all right, in hiding, it's *it* all right, Tragedy, it's stirring just a little, it's sending little ripples down the curtain . . .

But above all they mustn't, they mustn't at any cost allow the slightest suspicion . . . it's vital that they seem to be examining it with their undivided attention, with intense curiosity, as if it were a very stable, very firm, very solid object . . . nothing that could remind anyone of a curtain, of a veil that sends shudders, shivers . . . they must keep perfect control of themselves, make not a single movement that might seem to be a violation, an intolerable violation of such admirable discretion, such perfect dignity.

Hence, from what remained deposited here, every so often—like bubbles in the water of an aquarium—silent laughter rises, bursts noiselessly . . . But they came in, and the aquarium was immediately transformed into an open space, full of air, of light, in which their laughter will ring out noisily, send great waves of gaiety breaking, rolling here . . . "Ah, you're someone who likes funny stories, I have a good one to tell you, stop me if you've already heard it . . . It's the story of the Japanese journalist . . . No? You're sure to like it . . . Just remembering it makes me laugh out loud . . . This journalist arrives in Peking and goes to interview . . ." They start laughing . . . "It *is* funny, isn't it? It's one of those anecdotes that makes me laugh the most . . . It's stupid, I can't help it, it makes me cry, look . . . you see, I'm crying with laughter . . ."

They look at those tears of laughter flowing, moistening his cheeks, and they think there are too many of them . . . too many tears . . . there must already have been a whole reservoir full of them, and now it has been breached, it's becoming drained, it's a torrent in which tears of laughter are mingled with tears . . . if they could just moisten a fingertip with a few drops and taste them, they would, they are sure, taste of . . . they know what they would taste of . . . yes, no doubt about it, those tears . . . they are bitter tears.

And then their laughter rings out so loudly . . . Doesn't it ring out too loudly? . . . enormous cascades of laughter . . . Isn't it what might be called hysterical laughter? the sort you sometimes hear at the scene of tragic accidents, disasters?

"Then the Japanese asks, with an innocent air . . ." they can't take their eyes away, they're a little anxious, tense . . . just a slight false movement, just a very brief pause, and the acrobat launching himself over the void won't be able to hang on, he'll fall, he'll crash down into what is there, underneath him, Tragedy, they can see him . . . a moment's hesitation . . . oh no though, he *is* hanging on . . . "Yes, so the Japanese asks: 'Have you never thought . . .' Ah, what a skillful trapeze artist, how calmly he swings, so much at ease on his bar . . . "So the Japanese, he asks: 'Have you never tried to give them . . .' What a relief to see him so tranquil, so secure . . . 'Wouldn't it be more effective to use cyanide?' . . ." "Ha ha ha, that's a very good one, that's very funny, that's really hilarious . . ."

But also, beforehand, what must they not have gone through? what uncomfortable moments . . .

When they leave here, they will imagine that they are leaving a sad clown behind them, sad like all clowns . . . they will picture him after he has finished his number, when he's taking off his makeup, removing the layer of greasepaint from his cheeks down which his tears have traced delicate grooves, dug narrow furrows.

Their hands on their chair arms, they half rise, they're about to stand up . . . and then no, not yet, they sit down again . . . Although this is certainly the moment when anywhere else . . . but not here, they haven't the heart to abandon him, to let him fall back, sink back into that somber, quivering mass from which they have managed to extricate him, they have kept him outside, on that ground strewn with ills of all sorts, but isolated, dispersed ills, which don't prevent the fact that what is there under their feet is still good, stable ground, solid, compact . . .

Just a moment, though . . . he might notice that we daren't leave him on his own, and there's probably nothing he would find more insufferable . . . it was to avoid that, to give the impression that he too felt he was on firm ground, that he made all those efforts . . . so many efforts . . . Perhaps he's so exhausted that all he wants is to be left to his own devices, to be able to let himself go, to sink into what is now his element, the only one it has become possible for him to live in . . .

However that may be, waiting, hesitating, dragging things out . . . what's the use? that's just "putting off the evil day" . . . So they take the plunge. "My goodness, whatever is the time? Do you realize what the time is? It's gone so quickly . . . we really must be going . . . Lord save us!" . . .

On their way back from here, it seems to them that something escaped from him, escaped from his gaze, his voice, his hand as it shook their hands . . . a timid, fearful appeal, a trembling distress signal . . . something he must have been secreting without realizing it . . . like threads that stick, that cling, that adhere . . . it's stayed fastened on to them, they take it off, they wipe themselves, they rub, has it gone? there's still just a slight trace, a very small stain, but you really have to know it's there to be able to see it, and it'll gradually disappear, it won't show any more.

"Death" . . . it's as if all of a sudden they are reeling, staggering, they don't know what to hang on to, they're having difficulty in keeping their balance . . . that's where it came from, a violent gust of wind, an explosion, it came from that word which one of them has just tossed in here . . . "Death" . . . it can only have come from that . . . "Death" . . . a word, though, which in their absence was able to circulate freely here without producing any such effect . . . a perfectly ordinary word in current usage here just as it is anywhere else . . . But never for a single second do they forget that they are not just anywhere else . . . Here, this word, however banal and inoffensive the way it is employed, this word in itself . . . "Death" . . . they know that here, no one must ever, in any circumstances . . . who doesn't know that one must not speak of a rope in the house of a hanged man?

And "Death" . . . however much, anywhere else, it may be a word that is just as common and functional as "rope," "Death," pronounced here, would immediately remind them of where they were, and would have exactly the same effect as if, in the house of a hanged man, someone pronounced the word "rope."

"Death" . . . they are shocked, they look in astonishment, rather pityingly, at the clumsy wretch who has suddenly . . . but how could he? but he can't have done it on purpose . . . No doubt, ever since he has been here he hasn't stopped seeing it, staring at it . . . "Death," the word that should have been avoided at all costs . . . He was like the learner-cyclist who never fails to bump into the obstacle he has been warned to be very careful of . . . which he has been trying his hardest to steer clear of . . .

"Death" . . . but it doesn't do any good to adopt an air of indifference, of inattention . . . they see it as they see the air adopted by courteous, hospitable hosts while the spilt water is being mopped up, the pieces of the broken vase are being picked up . . .

"Death" . . . some of them make a visible effort to show that they hadn't heard it, and they feel embarrassed, as in an invalid's sickroom when one of his visitors doesn't want to see the object brought in by the nurse, and discreetly, shamefacedly, averts his eyes.

"Death" . . . the blundering idiot who blurted out this word, forgetting how risky, how dangerous it is to try to repair the damage done by a blunder, is he now going to repeat the word "Death," this time in a jocular, lighthearted tone, as if he were showing a carnival mask placed over a roguish pink face? . . . all he'll manage to do is evoke with greater clarity a death mask covering a dead man's face. But he is too shrewd, too experienced, to run such a risk. He wants, on the contrary, to banish the word from here, he wants it to be forgotten, and he thinks he should search as far away from here as possible, he bestirs himself, he grabs something at random and brings it back here . . . but whatever was he getting at? . . . it's so bizarre, so unexpected and incongruous . . . all it does is reveal, is extend, is communicate his embarrassment, his disarray, to everyone . . .

How right they were when they didn't even try to vindicate themselves, when they didn't feel the least bit at fault . . . on the contrary, by refraining from coming here they demonstrated the "charity that begins at home," and which, what's more, ends at other people's homes.

# 13

"BOREDOM? REALLY?" "YES, WHAT THEY GIVE ME is a feeling of great boredom, mortal boredom." "Boredom" . . . how that word surprises . . . it has never been employed here, either when they were present or after they had gone, to cover whatever they may have produced here. No doubt it's one of those words for well-to-do, spoiled people who have sensitive palates, gourmets accustomed to great delicacies . . . or on the contrary for undernourished people who need a more fortifying kind of food to build them up . . .

But here . . . how can we trace all the beneficial effects they produce . . .

The moment they arrive, everything here immediately becomes exactly the sort of environment that suits them, their customary environment where they feel at home, in a smallish place surrounded by thick, hermetically sealed walls . . . like a concrete bunker . . . but why a bunker? for protection against what? against what dangers? what deadly raids? Seeing that from now on there's no danger, no trace left of fear, of apprehension, while they are profusely pouring out all they've brought with them, all the things that come from where they live, so many and such varied objects . . . "The wing and the rear door completely bashed in, one of the headlights broken, and it's brand-new, it was parked, luckily the insurance . . . but all that time wasted and just when we were about to go away . . ." "To go away? not for long? That's not where you go for your holidays . . ." the sunlit facade of a hotel appears, bungalows, palm trees, the fine sand on the beach, the transparent blue sea . . . "No, just to my parents, in the Oise . . ." and here are some meadows, an opaque river . . . "But now I come to think of it, tax returns have to be sent in before the first . . ." There are signs of slight panic, here . . . "Before the first? Are you sure? Hasn't it been extended until the fifth?" "No no . . . Actually, though, where did I put it? . . ." and here papers and files are flicked through, moved around . . . it'll turn up, it's bound to . . . the emotion is the sort you feel when you're driving in one of those little bumper cars . . . a lighthearted emotion, it's all right, here it is, a thick double sheet covered in pale blue characters, and the documents are there as well, all together, no need to go and check . . . and they have found theirs, too, you can see that by their satisfied, carefree look . . . And now what else have they brought? "Ah, children . . . what a dance they lead you . . ." "What can you do, it's an age . . ." they bring them in here, dressed in clothes that make them presentable, familiar . . . "The little girl has a mind of her own, she's always been pigheaded, like my poor mother . . . and her brother . . . well, he . . . you know what boys are like . . . football matches, boxing matches . . ."

All the walls of this hermetically sealed place gradually become covered . . . there's nothing that doesn't immediately find its place, nothing that you want to remove, nothing that jars . . . even those imitation flowers, in plaster, in painted metal . . . "In the end we gave up planting flowers . . . that way we only have to pull up the weeds every so often . . . Ah, if only we could go there more often . . . The stone is beautiful, but it's still too white." "You'll see, it'll turn into a lovely, nicely patinated gray . . ." "That's true, it takes time, I've been rubbing it with moss, but . . ."

All the walls here are completely papered over with these tiny little pictures which they had cut out, they fit into each other like the colored pieces of a jigsaw puzzle and make a big, motley fresco that runs all the way round and has unexpected, very varied details, not at all unsightly, even rather entertaining . . .

But they've gone, they've "vacated the premises," and this time, quite rightly, they've taken it all away with them, everything they brought, they never leave anything behind, no deposit, no trace, no suspicious stain that might become more visible, darker, bigger, that might cover everything . . . The walls they had built around them have disappeared with them . . .

All that is left behind them is the very clean, smooth, solid ground . . . and, escaping, taking off, moving away, rising higher and higher . . . what is it? no one ever speaks of it . . . it's true that it's difficult, where can the words be found? What can it be compared to? Perhaps to a completely hermetic, compact sphere . . . a celestial body . . . Alone . . . surrounded by a void . . . nothing within proximity, nothing that could approach it, reach it, brush against it . . .

Nothing from outside, however delightful it may be, can come and spread itself there, it's already packed, crammed, full up . . . full of what?

It possesses such intensity, such extraordinary power . . . the power of something that does nothing other than . . . nothing other than what? . . . nothing other than exist . . .

It's something invulnerable, it's invincible . . .

It's so light . . . like a very gentle breath, like a very gentle rustling . . .

That's what it is, yes, it's certainly that, it's here . . . eternity.

◈ ◈ ◈

Wouldn't it be amusing to see how they would look if one were to be so extremely foolish as to show them the beneficial effects that are sometimes produced here by those people who give them a feeling of such great, such mortal boredom.

# 14

"WHY?" . . . THIS IS THE FIRST TIME, NEVER UP to the present had "Why?" appeared . . . and now all of a sudden "Why . . . yes, why does he do that? . . ." a narrow shaft of light, a faint, flickering gleam at the end of a labyrinth . . . "Why?" at the end of a path strewn with pebbles. Pebbles that he dropped, that he left here behind him . . . big pebbles scattered at random . . . you tripped over each one of them, you stumbled, you hurt yourself . . . and now here they come like a succession of signs leading to that "Why?", that issue, that hope of deliverance . . .

But is it possible? Is there really a link between these different signs? Is each one really a staging post? That "Why?" gleaming at the far end, isn't it a hallucination, the result of lassitude, of a need to escape? Is it a fakir's rope or a real, solid rope . . . which, if you held on tightly to each of its knots one after the other, would enable you to hoist yourself up to the outside, up to a place where you would feel protected, where help will arrive, in which there may perhaps be an answer . . .

We need to see him again, and he mustn't come back in just any sort of order . . . initially he must present himself in the same light as when he came here for the first time, bringing such impressive letters of recommendation, being welcomed with every consideration, with all the prerogatives his activities and knowledge merited and, although his time is so precious, so useful, so much in demand, being quite happy to waste a little of it here . . .

Wasn't there anything, at that moment, even at that very first moment, that could have made it possible to foresee . . . when, with that air of calm assurance, he stated as a fact that he also took the same delight in frequenting other places than this, that he had another favorite place? . . . And the name of that place, as soon as he pronounced it . . . the name of one of those over-populated places, fortunately a long way away, one of those places that are best avoided . . . here, just their very name introduces something like the nauseating stench of stale air, the smell of cheap toilet water, of cheap beauty products . . . But these brief whiffs are immediately dispelled and he is completely enveloped, perfumed in delightful sincerity, his awkwardness is seen as being due to innocence, to his ignorance of how to humor people, of how to avoid wounding their pride

. . . Did anyone want there to be anything of that impurity in him, that scorn which would make him reluctant to admit to his tastes, rather strange tastes, very independent and very varied, so as to humor shameful, degrading susceptibilities which he doesn't see, which he can't be aware of? . . . "Yes, his books and yours . . . they're next to each other on my shelves . . . I like to go back to them . . . You don't know them . . . Is that possible? Well, I can recommend them to you . . ." And immediately here that acquiescence, that eagerness . . . "Yes, I certainly will, since you recommend them . . ."

And was there nothing there that could have given any inkling of . . . not a shadow, not a suspicion of "Why?" . . . nothing . . . really?

He must stay there, not be allowed to go . . . he must say it again . . . "You know, that's also very important for me, I like to go back there . . . it's like with you, I always place you side by side . . ."

Is it he again, this deformed little monster, misshapen but full of energy, who bounces in here as if he owned the place, as if he had conquered it . . . his suspicious gaze inspects . . . does anyone dare budge? "And you would have the nerve to move away from the row I assigned you, where I lined you up side by side? That isn't your place? You are somewhere else? A little higher up, perhaps? Aha, so you are nowhere?" "Oh no, don't think that . . ." "I knew it, you acquiesce, you are very sensibly going to fall into line of your own accord

. . . that's right . . . be sure to do so, you'll see, it's a proximity that cannot fail to be beneficial to you . . ."

Yes, here and nowhere else . . . He is perfectly well aware of the rules of etiquette, of decorum . . . It was only here where, the moment he arrived, he stamped his foot with such violence . . . Look, it's beginning to emerge, it's there, barely visible, it's so strange, unexpected, unknown . . . it's like a preliminary sketch . . . like the first knot on the rope . . . maybe you could hoist yourself up if you grabbed it and held fast . . . "Why? Yes, why does he do that?"

It's that word, that same word, which when repeated in a different tone of voice conjures up its second meaning, the opposite of the first, and the clash between the two meanings, their collision, produces an explosion which develops irresistibly into enormous explosions of laughter . . .

He is the only one who has not noticed this surprising outburst, provoked with such admirable skill . . . it was the second sense that reached him, that he grasps, that he squeezes . . . a sponge swollen with what is called cruelty, cynicism, the indifference of the affluent to the sufferings of others . . .

He passes it . . . a heavy, flabby sponge, over the remains of the bursts of laughter that have subsided and lie scattered on the ground, he wipes, he rubs everywhere . . . "How can anyone forget, joke about the misfortunes that have befallen a whole country, with an entire population victimized, terrorized, their shops empty, their pipes frozen . . ."

And here, we are dumbfounded . . . we look on in amazement . . . we were a thousand leagues away . . . it had disappeared, we had forgotten it . . . we cringe with shame . . . because it was so deafening, that explosion produced by the unexpected clash of two opposite meanings of the same word . . .

But this time he won't get away with it so easily . . . This time he has been summoned here to be examined as never before . . . Is he really so extraordinarily insensitive to humor, to the funny side of things, so incapable of admiring such ingenuity, such subtlety, that he dares to sweep away those poor fallen bursts of laughter which he brutally wiped out with his disinfectant products . . . compassion, sympathy, the consideration owed to the sufferings of others . . . But no, of course not, anywhere else he has never . . . it would be known . . . anywhere else he would be too afraid of appearing timid, slow-witted, narrow-minded . . . a spoilsport, a lummox . . . Anywhere else he too would probably, would certainly have been shaken with laughter . . .

But here, he has a tremendous urge to call us to order, to bring us to heel, this urge has completely taken him over, it weighs on him until he is full to bursting point, and he bursts . . . Why?

"Yes, you've already said that . . ." and here we feel embarrassed, contrite, we must be more vigilant, we must watch ourselves more carefully, we mustn't forget . . . if he didn't point it out, we would never notice that we are repeating ourselves . . .

But the thing is that inadvertently, as ill-luck would have it, we reoffended . . . Whereupon he pounces . . . "Definitely, it's an obsession with you."

At this, even here we falter slightly, we restrain ourselves, we clutch at straws, we ward him off as best we can . . . "But you know, that sort of remark is not very kind, not very polite . . ." He seems surprised . . . do we have to explain to him . . . to *him*? of course not, that would be ridiculous, he knows it better than anyone . . . a brief gesture . . . "That's not done" is enough.

But now that the effect has worn off and we are no longer dazed, reeling, now that he is going to remain here for as long as is necessary, we can take our time . . . "Definitely, it's an obsession with you" . . . Where did you get that from? Show us, it's interesting . . . what did you dig out here and take home with you, and then put together again? . . . You must possess a splendid collection, and now once again you've got hold of something from here to allow you to complete that collection, to give it a name: "Obsession." You never let anything pass, you never stop inspecting, you are so vigilant, curious, avid . . . You are the only one who is so much like that, no one else is, although there is something of the sort in quite a few people who come and go here, but you are the only one to have seen it, seized on it, taken it away . . . in any case, the only one who has taken the liberty of revealing it. Why?

But what we see now . . . it's going past again in slow motion . . . is even more difficult to understand . . . the way you looked when, awkwardly, feebly, clutching at straws, we tried to remind you with our "That's not done" . . . yes, *you* who know certain social conventions better than anyone . . . that curious transformation . . . you suddenly became a member of the proletariat, "and proud of it," a plebeian who has never been taught manners, who doesn't know what is or is not done in smart society where people have a certain bearing, a certain accent . . . yours suddenly changed when you repeated: "Aha, that isn't done . . . Aha, really? . . ." That bumptious tone, that drawl . . . where did you get them? Why?

◈ ◈

He can't contain himself any longer, he lets himself go, without the slightest qualms he pours out, he scatters everywhere around him here a whole lot of little bits of junk that he has brought back with him and is getting rid of . . . petty concerns, trivial worries, no matter what . . . he goes into the greatest detail about his trifling aches and pains . . . ingrowing toenails, corns, calluses, bunions, itches . . . without the slightest sense of shame, he even seems to take a delight in laying himself bare in this way, in wallowing in his lack of restraint, in being quite repugnant, as he isn't, as he cannot be, anywhere else, as he can never be anywhere other than here . . . But why, though? Why?

He stiffens, draws back, already takes up a position from which he can reject whatever we may be going to offer him . . . But he won't be able to manage it this time, it's too fascinating, irresistible, he'll be forced to lean forward, he'll grasp it, hold it, help to keep it here, in the center, so that it can be sized up, examined from all sides, it'll be interesting, exciting to see new details, unexpected aspects begin to emerge, become visible when we all start observing it closely together . . . But even this time he refuses to look at it, he kicks it away, or else he picks it up for a moment and then casually drops it again, with such an air . . . an air of what? . . . an air of boredom, of contempt, which he flaunts, which he accentuates, he wants to make quite sure that we see it . . . Why?

And so, from "Why" to "Why," clinging on to each one of them, we arrive . . . but in what a strange place . . . a strange, foreign place that is nothing like here . . . Yes, though, it's like in our dreams, when we are absolutely certain that the person who appears under the guise of a stranger is actually someone familiar, someone very close . . . it really is that same person, it's he, we know it, we aren't even surprised . . . and what we see now, which is nothing like, but absolutely nothing like here, which has never looked like that, it really is here, there's no doubt about it, the same here that is crisscrossed by currents, that is open to the four winds, shapeless, formless . . .

It really is the same here, this monument, this enormous palace, it really is the same name, that name that here shows to the outside world, that is carved on its pediment . . . the people who stand in front of its imposing facade, in front of its lofty, closed gates, know that they'll never get permission to visit it, they know that that is a favor, a reward only granted to the chosen few, those few rare initiates who have proved themselves capable of appreciating the treasures it contains . . . And they, who are they to deserve? . . . They know they will never have that luck . . .

But he . . . who would believe it? who could ever imagine it? he, who looks as if he is one of them, all he has to do is give them a little kick, and the gates open for him . . .

He feels the impact on him of something coming from the glances of the people who are left outside, something like a current generated by their astonishment, their nostalgia, their envy, a powerful current that presses on him, controls all his movements, makes him act in strange ways . . . His hand held out in casual, familiar fashion, his eyes sending a glance over this unique place . . . but it isn't unique for him . . . there is another place he likes just as much, it may perhaps be less imposing, but he sees no difference between the two, and he immediately says so, he announces it very loudly as if he were paying a compliment, and his words are listened to, yes, in that place, would you believe it, you people out there, those words that come from me are accepted, absorbed in a silence suffused with interest, with deference, with modesty . . .

And just see how they crowd round me to entertain me, to please me . . . to get me to listen to that amazing clash between two opposite meanings of the same word . . . and naturally I notice that explosion, but those subsequent explosions of laughter which the first one spread around it by contagion are not at all to my liking, you know, so I put an abrupt stop to them in the name of the rules of morality, of decency . . . and you see how they immediately cringe, look crestfallen, contrite . . .

There, where no one ever enters except on tiptoe, taking great care not to bump into anything, not to make a mess of anything, I . . . it even surprises *me*, sometimes . . . I sprawl all over the place, I wallow . . .

How disdainfully I reject their offerings, which would overwhelm anyone else, or at any rate every one of you out there, and then you can see how upset, how disappointed they are as they take them back, they search . . .

I pronounce final judgments, I pass harsh sentences . . . And when I perceive, but this is very rare, a timid movement of rebellion, an attempt at resistance, I crush it, I pulverize it with a heavy, greasy, viscous, dribbling accent . . .

Where is the prestigious place that could give me such an exciting sense of my exceptional, extraordinary power . . .

But sometimes, too, when I am outside, among you, mingling with you, looking just like you, when I am one of those who keep their eyes raised up to that inaccessible high place and I am listening to their naive, admiring, respectful remarks while I say not a word, while I keep my secret to myself, what rare, incomparable joy, what subtle voluptuous pleasure I feel at being there, alone, alone in the knowledge that I am completely at home up there, that there I do whatever I like.

So that was what it was, that so promising light at the end of the labyrinth . . . That was where they led, to those laborious journeys, those return trips, those efforts to manage to hoist oneself up from "Why" to "Why."

It was to gain access to them, to those dismal regions in which subjugated populations live surrounded by imposing monuments crudely constructed with shoddy materials in conformity with the most banal conventions . . .

What's the use of persevering, of trying to go any farther into places where for as far as the eye can reach there is nothing but such constructions? Is there the slightest chance of finding anything there that would not be just as disappointing . . .

# 15

THAT SILENCE . . . YES, IT WAS WHAT IS CALLED silence . . . it was never called that here, it had no name . . . but now that it's returning . . . a form vaguely emerging . . . that's the name it appears under: Silence . . . Lost and almost forgotten, it is returning home from far-off countries, showing a passport issued there, in foreign parts, specifying that name: Silence.

"Silence" . . . What other name could be given to that absence of any words exchanged between two people alone together, what could anyone observing them say other than "they are remaining silent." And it must be recognized that of all the very many, very different kinds of silence . . . there'd be no end to it if we tried to mention them all . . . that particular sort is one of those with a rather bad reputation . . .

When the two people who aren't speaking look as if

they have known each other intimately for a long time and the silence between them is prolonged, to anyone outside who stops, who lingers, it often communicates a sense of remoteness, of weariness, of boredom, of "the loneliness of a couple," which we know can be even more painful than the other sort . . .

"Silence" . . . did it really have to come back from so far away, did it really have to be gone for so long before it revealed itself, still masquerading under that name, exposed to foreign gazes, making this or that impression, deserving this or that reputation . . .

It did finally return, how could it not have returned, drawn in, sucked in by such a long wait, it's here again just as it was before . . . under its pressure that name, "Silence," has cracked up, fallen apart, disappeared . . . there's no longer any name for what is here, which fills everything . . . something that came to add itself, no though, it didn't add itself, it melted, merged into what was already here . . . it's one single indivisible substance, all of a piece.

What word here could leap up . . . where from? to land where? on to what other side? on to what other bank? There is no other side, there are no other banks, there is no space to cross, nothing to make one's way toward, nothing to reach, nothing to meet . . .

It's immeasurable, limitless, you never know how far it may extend . . .

The slightest little parcel of land, no matter how tiny, how humble, how insignificant, when it alights there . . . what has just appeared, what remains there, that little bit of the grassy path along that old gray wall . . . is as indispensable as, is even more indispensable than, the vastest, most immense part of the world . . . that substance which fills everything here, where it has come and taken root, nourishes it, gives it a radiance, an affirmative force, an extraordinary assurance . . . It seems as if what was floating everywhere, scattered, diluted, has come to settle, to be concentrated in that little bit of grassy path . . . it has become something very resistant, indestructible. The precise point that contains in condensed form everything that exists of certainty, of security.

If words, if even a single word were suddenly to arrive as it might arrive anywhere, coming from the permanently available common stock, it would seem to have been propelled automatically, by accident, to have escaped from some mechanism that had suddenly gone wrong. It would destroy, it would transform, it would convert here into a strictly demarcated space, hardened, flattened, leveled and marked out, and covered with motorways and railtracks where words circulate, where they cross known, scheduled distances that connect one place to another.

But isn't this one of those images conjured up to reinforce, to make even more delightful, our confidence that nothing of that sort could ever happen here . . . No mechanism exists here that could go wrong or from which even by accident such a word could be propelled . . .

No contraption of that kind could penetrate into what is out of its reach, unattainable . . . inviolable . . .

It seems as if somewhere far in the background, very far away, there are sort of very faint flickers . . . barely perceptible . . . sort of gleams, glows . . .

It seems as if a little mirror here is capturing the sun's rays and bringing flecks of light into play on the horizon, creating fleeting glimmers . . .

It seems as if a warmth is spreading from here to somewhere very far away and gradually heating, helping to germinate, to bud . . . words will spring up from it and come and alight here in this soil . . . there is none, there can be none more favorable to them . . .

◇ ◇

But of course not, above all not that, especially not now, while all that is still very far away . . . a vibration, a very faint flickering, a quivering, a fluttering, the trembling of something uncertain, hesitating on the verge of existence.

There must be no hope, no promise to set it in motion, to make it spring up, leap up in an attempt to reach, whatever the cost, to get hold of something that will grow, swell, take to the air, glide . . .

And then—you never know—just one tiny little hole is enough, a hole just as small as the one made by the point of a needle, to pierce it, to empty it, to make it fall to the ground, collapse, lie flat . . . the shriveled remains of a crumpled little balloon . . .

There must be no virtualities, no possibilities harbored in it to let it fortify itself, stretch itself, send out in every direction, against all opposition, powerful, prehensile branches.

There must be no expectation to allow it to stretch out surreptitiously, fearfully, with the avidity of the famished . . .

And no premonition . . . Heaven could punish such presumption . . .

There must be nothing there that moves, nothing must ripen, eject, project as far as here . . . here must remain pure of all words . . .

There must be the possibility of watching what appears and disappears there, as one watches a fleeting glimmer, a flash of heat lightning . . .

There must be nothing that in however small a way could harm this sense of fulfillment, that could to the slightest extent cloud this serenity . . .

Just only for this time . . .

# 16

If Adam and Eve had only known what was in store for them when God allowed them the knowledge of good and evil, if they'd known that they would never be able to prevent themselves from immediately seeing and distinguishing between good and evil everywhere, and since God had created them in his own image, from distinguishing them even to such a point, even to the infinitely small . . .

What could be more infinitesimal than what has just appeared on the screen, in that palace stateroom where the new head of government is passing down the serried ranks of the men from whom he may perhaps make his choice, shaking each one's hand . . . and each one with diffidence, with dignity, with the correct air of detachment, shakes his hand and looks at him . . . and then there is one particular man . . . is it in the motion of his arm which rises just that little bit too quickly, or in the movement of his neck which stretches just those few centimeters too far forward, a thin, flexible neck which oscillates too easily, or in the corner of his eye, of his eyelid, of his lip . . . there's no mistaking it . . . a tiny little particle, an infinitesimal quantity of something has crept out from somewhere there, has spread, and caused this slight uneasiness here . . . There's no time, there's no need to try to see where it comes from, to break it down into its elements, to name them, it's immediately obvious, and to everyone, that it's evil . . . but what sort of evil, exactly? If it had to be shown to people who weren't there to see it, it would have to be broken down, named . . . it was avidity, covetousness, humility, cowardice, sycophancy . . . but however hard one tried, one could never manage to define everything that that evil was made up of.

And even more minute was what appeared while we were casually chatting round the garden table, under the tree in blossom, on the soft grass, when someone mentioned the unexpected promotion of . . . of who was it again? but it doesn't matter . . . that movement in him, that slight movement which everyone there noticed, the ripple, the wave that emanated from him and unfurled here . . . did it come from his astonishment? no, it wasn't that, everyone recognized it, everyone could have tried to give it a name if it had been necessary . . . later, they were all able to recall it to convince themselves that they had not been mistaken . . . yes, it had contained something that could be called suspicion, hostility, jealousy, envy . . . and then immediately afterward, almost simultaneously, there, in that smile, in that look exhibiting satisfaction, goodwill, there was something that made it, the action of that particle of evil, even more pernicious, even more virulent . . . it was also made up of shiftiness, of hypocrisy . . .

Are they not curious, the effects that even a very faint trace of evil produces, as mysterious as those produced by swallowing those tiny little pills made according to the principles of homoeopathy . . .

But what about little particles of good? Don't we feel them? Of course we do, immediately, and in equally minute quantities . . . in a look, in the curve of a lip, of an eyelid, of a cheek . . . the silent wave that radiates from them, you can't say exactly what it contains, everyone notices it, recognizes it . . . that reflection in the other person of a sorrow, of a joy . . . sharing between brothers . . . well, something benevolent, a particle of good . . .

Only it must be acknowledged that neither the gentle caress from a passing breeze, nor the reassuring reminder that good is there, ever-present, ever-possible, produces effects comparable in strength and duration to those produced by equally tiny amounts of evil.

And how strange it is, that presence . . . always there, standing in a corner, that statue . . . the statue of good, of perfect good . . . of absolute perfection . . . every single one of its numerous, innumerable facets is made of a homogeneous substance, nothing could be more pure . . . Or more fragile . . . just the slightest scratch sends a network of fine cracks running over it, spreading, covering it . . .

That particular facet, all disinterestedness, perfect detachment, perfect dignity, of the same nature and the same quality as what, in other circumstances, we admire in heroes and saints . . . all of a sudden a barely perceptible current has made that arm rise a bit too quickly, that neck stretch forward a little bit too far, it has produced a twitch at the corner of that eyelid, of that lip, and the whole facet has become damaged, scarred, it has fractured, disintegrated, broken . . . and the hole that replaced it has been filled with something dubious, dirty, with impurity itself . . . a rather revolting mixture . . . of avidity? of cowardice? of baseness? . . . well, who doesn't know what it is? . . . no one could mistake it . . .

the thing that came and embedded itself there was a particle of evil.

And when it happens that one facet of this statue of absolute perfection is grazed, however slightly, let's say the facet of the love of one's neighbor, of perfect brotherhood, it begins to shine more brightly, to radiate . . . And doesn't the thing that came to throw light on it make one think of the very gentle, very soothing flicker of one of those little flames that illuminate sacred images and pious objects?

# 17

WITH THOSE PEOPLE, THOUGH, IT SHOULD HAVE gone without saying that that expression is insufferable, that it really is one of those that give you the creeps . . .

But what's the matter with them? Where do they get it from, that discomfited, disconcerted air, you'd think they were afraid to commit themselves, they wonder, they hesitate . . . at last they decide . . . "Oh, you know, there are so many people who use that expression . . ."

"There are so many . . ." that produced a tremor here, like a minor explosion . . . the object that had been chosen, not even chosen, but touched at random and picked up out of so many others which could be shown to them to entertain them, to make them feel at home, to remind them . . . but didn't they already know it?... that here we respond to the same things, that "we speak the same language" . . . That object was dangerous, a booby trap that had never been defused, it exploded . . . A small explosion . . . and what came bursting out of it was "There are so many."

Instantly, everything here is transformed, everything shrinks, it seems as if everything has been covered in an unbroken coat of plaster . . . we are squeezed in between rock-hard walls which are completely sealed . . . not the slightest little crack . . .

"There are so many" . . . a dense, compact crowd has invaded everything, it surrounds them, encloses them, carries them, and that expression has just arrived in their midst, it circulates, it passes from hand to hand, after so much handling it has become rounded, polished, it's a little ball that they themselves must have caught and passed on without feeling anything, without paying attention to it, they can't withdraw it from circulation, step aside, go off into a corner to study it, they wouldn't be able to even if they wanted to, but they don't want to . . . What's the good of making such an effort? What's the point? "Oh, you know, there are so many people who use that expression, it's nothing to get excited about . . . There are more important things . . ."

More important than that? But what in the world can be more important than "There are so many"?

Whatever the cost, something must be extracted from this melee, forced out, even if it's only a . . . "You, yes you, look, get hold of this expression, hold it tight, try to keep a grip on it . . . Can it be possible that you don't feel . . . There's something there, isn't there?" . . . But he doesn't even try to get hold of it, he turns away, retreats, it's as if he had been sucked up, absorbed by the enormous mass, he's going to melt into it, he's disappearing . . .

It's painful to have to do it, but it must be done . . . there's something stirring there, it's still alive, it hasn't yet been completely crushed, annihilated, it can still be saved . . . But to use such means . . . to hurl that against that peaceful multitude, all huddled up together in reassuring warmth . . . tranquillity, security is all they ask . . . to hurl that against all those defenseless, rather flabby, out-of-condition bodies, all with one accord nodding assent with their placid, ingenuous faces, repeating in docile fashion "There are so many . . . There are so many . . ."

⟡ ⟡

But there can be no further hesitation, it's "a question of life and death," and here it comes, it's released, it's on its way . . . "What does that prove?"

"What does that prove?" rumbles deafeningly above them . . . "What does that prove?" makes them crouch down, prostrate themselves, they send fearful glances up at the thing flying over them . . .

"What does that prove?" . . . a device coming from a distant, foreign arsenal . . . they weren't prepared, they hadn't learned how to protect themselves from it, they have no means of defence, no weapon which would allow them . . . some of them try to stand up, and there, within their reach, they find . . . they capture it, pick it up . . . "That proves . . . that proves . . ." but it's too heavy for them, they don't know how to handle it . . . "That proves . . . that proves . . ." no, they don't know how to use it, they drop it . . .

And now some of them are trying to restore a little calm . . . they warn the imprudent ones who might think themselves strong enough to recapture "That proves . . ." "Whatever you do don't touch it, it's too dangerous, leave it where it is, that 'that proves' . . . don't forget that 'just one' is enough, remember those exclusions, persecutions, condemnations which that 'just one' suffered, and then how, afterward, there were so many, so very many, not against it but for it . . . Take this one, rather, hoist it up: 'There are so many' cannot prove anything . . . 'There are so many'—we said that without thinking, out of laziness, inadvertence, oversight— 'There are so many,' it's obvious . . . hold it really high up, wave it about . . . 'There are so many' doesn't prove anything."

After having secured, even by such means, the surrender of these peaceful, innocent people, it is impossible not to take advantage of it by getting hold of some of them, taking them by the shoulders, forcing them . . . "Acknowledge, now, that there is something there . . . you can feel it . . ."

They agree . . . Yes, of course, they do feel it . . . "There's something in that expression . . . you can't deny it . . ." No no, they don't deny it, they acknowledge it . . . only they can't help it, they can't stop themselves trying to retreat imperceptibly so as to avoid as far as possible becoming contaminated by something amorphous, slightly flabby, gluey, which is oozing out of it, they suppress an urge to clean themselves up, because after all no one could be more cleanly than they, no one could be more particular about personal hygiene . . . they accept it under protest . . . "Yes, it's true, it really does have to be said that in that expression . . ." Then what happens here . . . grotesque, indecent . . . is cries, whoops . . . "Don't say it so grudgingly . . . don't try and hide your repugnance, your disdain . . . the thing that's there, the thing that's stirring, it's so fragile, so threatened, barely discernible . . . just a quivering, a fluttering . . . it deserves, do you hear, a great deal of consideration, of care, it deserves . . ." They make themselves small, they turn their eyes away apprehensively . . . "Well yes, the very thing you're spurning, it's, you understand, it's . . ." They daren't put their fingers in their ears in case they inflame him further, this maniac, he's going to choke . . . "What's there is, is . . ." Fury—or is it a sudden access of discretion?—prevents him from finishing.

How, after such a performance, after such splendid results, could he not regret, while there was still time, that he hadn't been willing to listen to them when they so wisely, so sensibly, advised him to concentrate on more important things?

# 18

IMMEDIATELY AFTER THAT "HOW ARE YOU?" . . . what could be more natural, though, more predictable . . . you feel a withdrawal, a contraction in the other . . . he propels a little too loudly, as if to push away . . . as if to protect himself . . . a "Very well, thank you," and even a "But very well, thank you" which is almost aggressive, perhaps involuntary and at once regretted, and then forces out the "Very well, thank you" even more loudly, to drive even farther away . . . thus demonstrating even more clearly that in the "How are you?" he had detected something which, however infinitesimal, barely discernible, immediately showed him that what he had been watching out for, dreading, fleeing, was indeed here . . . Not the slightest possible doubt: here, we *knew*.

Yes, it's true, here we do know it, but here isn't one of those places you must be in the habit of frequenting, it's even rather upsetting that you could have made such a great mistake . . . The fact of knowing it couldn't elicit words like "ditched," "chucked," words from elsewhere, the sort of degrading words which, here, only degrade those who use them.

But that furtive movement, that contraction, that frightened withdrawal . . . they arouse the need . . . which is never aroused by anything that is shielded from molestation, protected by its immobility, its independence . . . the need to approach, to touch, to grasp the thing that draws back, tries to hide, fearful, trembling . . . the irrepressible desire to take hold of it, to caress it gently, don't tremble, you have nothing to fear, there is no trace here of what you dread, nothing that can wound you, debase you, elevate itself at your expense, there is only the desire to help you, it's painful, unbearable to feel the extent to which here, in these friendly surroundings, you lack confidence . . .

But how to go about reaching you? With what words? Words that wouldn't make you withdraw even further into yourself, make you cower even further away, flee, escape, and never come back . . .

What are they, suddenly, these words that have emerged automatically, that arrived by themselves, the sort of words that are always holding themselves in readiness and which, the moment something from outside attracts them, get through quite naturally without having to submit to inspection . . . "You look wonderful. You look as if you're in great form . . ."

Then, as was only to be expected, they are received with a "Thank you" brought up from those distant, frozen regions where the wind of courtesy blows, the sort that "casts a chill," that leaves the people it has blown on shivering all over.

No word, from now on, will get through without having been carefully inspected.

The words file past prudently, sensibly, they cover vast spaces without enthusiasm . . . they wander lazily from one end of the world to the other . . . words with a rather insipid taste, they make you think of "low-calorie" food . . . they lack nourishing, fortifying ingredients, "their heart isn't in it."

But there, in that place . . . although wouldn't it be strange, incongruous, to place oneself there, to stop there . . . ah well, so what, "nothing venture, nothing win" . . . an incantation that has so often given people strength . . . "Don't you think it's funny . . . in the midst of all these events, of all these upheavals, this excitement, and not only in the popular press but also in the 'quality' newspapers, a revolting scandal . . . that most prestigious prince charming, he was spoiled for choice but he turned down the paragon of all the most admired qualities in favor of the most mediocre . . ." One more bit of daring, one more "nothing venture," find the courage to steer the words into this very exposed, dangerous side road . . . "Doesn't it seem like a choice in a competition, you'd think the loser hadn't deserved *that*, you'd think it unfair . . . Isn't it absurd? Isn't it unreal, childish? And that it should be so widespread . . ."

For a moment the lucky man, proudly basking in this admiration, after he had imagined himself rejected, dismissed into the pitiful ranks of the failures, is going to wake up, to shake himself, so after all it wasn't true, it was a nightmare, there hadn't been any failure, any debasement, anything that could be despised, anything that people could pity . . .

He's going to recover, it wasn't true, it was a bad dream . . . "Obviously they're completely ridiculous, whether favorable or unfavorable, these value judgments in a domain in which God knows . . ."

Yet nothing in him seems to have budged, his eyes express indifference, something like contempt . . . "I must say that for me, that kind of thing . . . I didn't follow it very closely . . . I've never been able to take much interest . . . I know, I have friends who, no one would ever believe it . . . well, the gossip columns and even romantic fiction . . . but personally . . ." "Oh, nor do I, you know, but this time there was all that publicity everywhere, all that indignation . . ."

So we shall have to start again, abandon those barren fields . . . maybe with patience, with luck, we'll manage to find . . .

It looks as if more suitable places are already beginning to appear in the distance . . . but we must be careful not to get there too soon, to take our precautions and then, after a fairly long and prudent journey, as soon as we get to that fertile, well-protected region, stop there . . . "It's always amazing, isn't it, when you come to think about it, that it took so many struggles, so many efforts, to get slaves, pariahs, to stop despising themselves and even to retaliate by despising those who despise them . . . by feeling superior to them, superior to those inferior, insensitive, uncouth individuals . . . I shall never forget the sight, years ago, in a theater in Harlem where no white American ever ventured, we were the only two whites there—obviously foreigners—when on the stage the actors, all blacks, chanted in chorus and were joined by the entire audience: 'Black is beautiful. White is ugly. U. G. L. Y. Ugly.' It was rather exhilarating, don't you think, this reversal of a tendency we all share?"

Doesn't it begin to look as if . . . or is it just crazy wishful thinking that produces this illusion . . . It begins to look as if he *is* recovering . . . doesn't he now see the person in front of him as a despicable, vulgar individual, unworthy of him . . .

Or maybe not, not really, isn't it rather the certainty that nothing in him can succeed in destroying, diminishing . . . isn't it the pride of knowing that anyone who chose him, who was chosen by him, could only, whatever happens, be of very high, very rare quality . . .

How to discover where it came from, that recovery? And *was* there one, even? It's useless to search these words . . . "Yes, it really is most amazing, the strength of the prejudices that succeed in contaminating the victims themselves . . ." Impossible to find anything in that rather stilted, inscrutable phrase of impeccable conformism, respectability . . .

In no time at all it disappeared, that need to reach, to capture, to hold, to caress, to soothe what is trembling, watchful, inside you, ever ready to run away and hide, to cower in the shadows.

But while the conversation is continuing on its course in all security, tranquilly, normally, the turmoil in the background here is all the time intensifying, it has become a veritable tumult . . . words loom up, jostle one another, push and shove, impatient words that haven't time to combine into phrases . . . isolated, incoherent words . . . "Perfect reciprocity . . . The horizontal bar of a swing . . . everyone always facing each other on the same level . . . Communicating vessels . . ." the words are going to come out and, on contact with the outside, become calculations, shabby tricks, precepts decreed by dolts . . .

But there's nothing to be afraid of, they won't come out.

◈ ◈

While the conversation is proceeding, a star can be seen hovering very high up over this dreary procession, a star surrounded by mists . . . it has its unknown laws, its strange movements . . . There, beyond every gaze, the pure water of living springs wells up, flows, ramifies, swells, runs dry . . . the words trying to get through will be soaring balloons, distended by the tone of the visionary, the mystic . . .

But they won't be able to get through.

Now, urged on by indignation, the words press harder, they're going to come pouring out . . . "You have profaned, debased, you have brought down and deposited here all this bric-a-brac . . . platforms, mikes, awards ceremonies, successes, failures, petty victories, falls, degradations, humiliations . . ."

But none of these insane words will be able to burst in, the conversation will continue, normally and calmly.

Only, what you thought you detected when you came in and were greeted by that inoffensive "How are you?", what made you shudder, draw back, is still there, there's no way to keep it at bay, it has managed to get through, to insinuate itself into that "Goodbye, keep well."

# 19

"WELL YES, SOME PEOPLE DO LEAVE YOU GASPING for air" . . . That was all it had been possible to get out of him, even though he is one of the very rare people whom one can venture to talk to about such things, can dare to ask whether he too . . . whether this had never happened to him . . . "It's so strange, you think it could never have happened to anyone . . . people . . . you don't know how . . . there's nothing in them that can help you to understand it . . . when they're there, and even quite some time after they are no longer there . . . they have an effect on you . . . how to put it . . . it's as if you no longer existed, no, that's not it, you do exist, but it isn't what used to be called existing . . . you are . . . you understand . . ." And he interrupted this gibberish, he said: "Ah yes, I know. Some people do leave you gasping for air" . . .

◈ ◈

"They leave you gasping for air" . . . words you want to reject, no, that's not it, not it at all . . . but they resist, they stay there, offering, throwing you a line which you clutch at, you don't know why . . . "They leave you gasping for air" . . . and, looming up through the thick fog, a real pea-souper, you see these words which make you perceive—really perceive? or in any case which make you think you perceive—that there is no air left in you for anyone to suck out of you, your own air has disappeared, it's as if you had never had any, not the slightest trace of it remains, there's nothing but the air in which you live, like them, a natural element that no more belongs to you than it does to anyone else . . . And you would never have noticed it, you would always have lived in it, you would still be in it at this moment . . .

But all of a sudden . . . how did it arrive? . . . there are little puffs, this is the air that belongs here, which was here before, it has come back . . . everything is stirring, quivering, the slightest stimulus produces waves that endlessly reproduce themselves . . . the most banal, well-worn, worn-out object suddenly, as if it is totally new, surprises you, fills you with wonder, troubles you, disturbs you, sometimes for a long while . . . the antennae, the tentacles, the suckers of words stretch out, search, feel, try to get hold . . .

Something has happened . . . there's an atrophy, an immobility . . . a sort of absence . . . Where were we? What is happening?

◈ ◈ ◈

How can we know? How can we manage to get hold of it? With what means? What words? There weren't any, over there, there was no one to feel it, to try to grasp it . . .

But it must be recovered at all costs. No question of giving up.

Well, never mind, there's no choice. There are no other means than those we have at our disposal. Inappropriate, inadequate words. Like "leave you gasping for air."

And if, by a bit of luck once again, as there was with "leave you gasping for air," unsuitable words could reveal . . . or at least hint at . . .

Then why not start with these—the first words that come naturally . . . "They arrived one fine day and installed themselves" . . .

But as "installed" won't do, nor, even, will "arrived" . . . seeing that their arrival was so immediately eclipsed . . . and everything that was here immediately disappeared with it, you might have thought it had never existed . . .

It was nevertheless their arrival that drove out the air that was here before, and replaced it . . . No . . . They didn't drive anything out, the air that had filled everything here was not imported air. It was quite simply air. There wasn't, there couldn't have been, any other.

But even so, it was with them that the air came in.

No. "Came in" might give the impression that it arrived from outside . . .

From what outside? There had been nothing else anywhere, other than what was there. Just as obvious, just as certain as the change in the seasons, the state of the weather, sunrise, or moonlight.

As obvious? as certain? Words like "obviousness," like "certainty," words that could bring them in and put them down on what was already there? And even "there" won't do. Where is there? There in relation to what?

"We were following the beaten track." Not at all, there were no beaten tracks. Beaten by whom? We walked anywhere we wanted. We could go wherever we liked.

"We were obeying the rules." No. What rules, if not the invisible, ineluctable, necessary ones that must regulate everything that exists.

Objects appeared . . . Objects that could arouse interest . . . Interest? But interest would have produced movements to help us become closer to these objects, to take hold of them, to grasp them, to try to squeeze goodness knows what out of them . . . but they passed by, unapproachable, untouchable, out of reach, they couldn't trigger any movement.

And now, as if caught up in the game, words arrive, barrier-words, just to amuse themselves by pressing a bit harder, hinting even more broadly . . . "Locked up" . . . Oh no. "Self-contained world" . . . No, obviously not. "Suffocation." No. "Boredom," no no. "Nostalgia." No, no and no. Nothing of that sort. Yes but what, then? Something that has existed, but all we can manage to do is catch a glimpse of what it was not.

But what on earth can that have come from—"what it was not"? An unknown substance has been absorbed . . . invisible, colorless, odorless . . . which has acted we don't know how, and caused this lethargy. This paralysis. This coma. This death.

What's the use of trying to recover it with the words of life?

# 20

NO, NOT THEM, NOT THOSE WORDS, THEY MUST stay where they are, in a safe place, well protected. Even the so natural, so usual desire to share with other people, to contemplate such treasures with them, couldn't incite us to exhibit them . . . every gaze, however appreciative, admiring, that falls on them, every slight touch, however delicate, respectful, and full of devotion it might be, would be unbearable, an intolerable intrusion, a profanation.

And as for the dread of one day seeing someone introduce them . . . Someone who would make himself ridiculous by presenting them, those words, by bringing them out from where they were found, shut away between the covers of old schoolbooks, parading on innumerable copies of homework and exam papers, constantly checked, scrutinized, turned over and over . . . Someone who, so as to air them a little, to give them an outing, would try to bring them here, still dressed in their unattractive school uniform, rather gauche, not knowing how to behave or what attitude to adopt, to those places which they aren't used to frequenting, to which they have never been invited . . . Wouldn't awkwardness, timidity, produce something in the tone in which they were introduced, something vaguely risible . . . and perhaps—how to avoid it? they can so easily lend themselves to it—a certain solemnity . . . wouldn't they give their syllables, rather too drawn out, too spaced out, an air of grandiloquence, of tragic exaggeration . . . "The eternal silence of those infinite spaces terrifies me" . . . Or else, on the contrary, so as not to let them linger, squash them up one against the other, jostle them, make them come tumbling out . . .

No no, we mustn't imagine things, we mustn't be afraid of anything of that sort . . . not for them, not for those words. They can rest here, unattainable, inviolable . . . here, they are perfectly safe.

When they arise, it is one of those rare moments when every impurity disappears from here, the tiniest little obstacle that might in any way hamper them, impede their movement . . .

And so they arrive . . . and doesn't it seem that at their approach everything revives, starts to vibrate . . . they resurface from those depths into which they one day fell, and deploy themselves . . . "The eternal silence of those infinite spaces terrifies me."

Words that resound noiselessly, they have come from nowhere, are addressed to no one, are pronounced in no other tone than their own tone, created by them, the only tone that can be perfectly true to them, in perfect conformity with what they are . . .

"The eternal silence of those infinite spaces terrifies me." The form of each word, the distance between them, the most precise distance possible, allows each one of them to grow, to stretch, and then on contact with the one that follows it to dilate, to expand even further, to soar ever higher, still higher, endlessly . . .

And everything here, borne by those words, wholly adhering to them, dilates, stretches, expands, rises . . . up to where? . . . you can stand it no longer, your courage fails . . .

And then when, carried up to a place from which no farther advance is possible . . . "terrifies me" falls . . . "terrifies me" . . . the quivering of a little bird shot down in full flight, lying motionless on the ground . . . "terrifies me" . . . the fluttering of its wings, still warm, living . . .

It really seems that that was the day when it appeared for the first time . . . not all of it, just a little bit, barely glimpsed . . . it was when we had been playing that amusing new game . . . you had to line up in the right order and without making any mistakes Monday, Tuesday, Wednesday, Thursday, Friday, Saturday, Sunday . . . and then start all over again Monday, Tuesday . . .

They come automatically now, they follow each other more and more quickly . . . Monday, Tuesday, Wednesday . . . "There's no point in going on . . ." "Yes, but then what, what comes next? again Monday, Tuesday? . . . and then what? again Monday, Tuesday, Wednesday, Thursday . . . and then Monday again? but for how long?" . . . "Forever."

Forever? . . . *Toujours*? . . . There's no way, even when you're trying your hardest, in which you can grasp what that word means, but there are so many things a child can't understand . . . you'll have to wait, for that as well, until you're grown up . . .

But in the meantime, it's such a funny word . . . it's amusing to pronounce it, to repeat it . . . for-ever . . . *tou-jours*, pushing your lips out, pursing them, like when you're going to whisper . . . *tou-jours* . . .

*Toujours* . . . like the soft, caressing words of lullabies which soothe, reassure . . . *tou-jours* . . . *tou-jours* . . .

Sometimes, when it's so good to find yourself beneath the starry vault, and find all the familiar stars exactly where they should be, you suddenly feel a presence behind them . . . something is there . . . barely visible, very dark, amorphous, limitless . . . if you tried to reach it, if you approached it, you would be sucked up, swept up, a feather in the wind, spiraling, absorbed, dissolved . . .

Quick, draw back, flatten yourself as hard as you can on the solid earth, your gaze riveted on the heavenly vault . . . And it once again closes up, becomes completely occluded, not the slightest porosity through which anything could infiltrate . . . nothing unsayable, nothing unbearable can insinuate itself into the peaceful scintillation of the heavenly bodies.

"The eternal silence of those infinite spaces terrifies me" . . . words that have really dropped from heaven . . . But of course not, they come from the earth . . . what could be more banal, more ordinary, than "silence," "infinite," "space," "eternal"? It needed a miracle to assemble them . . . no human will could have done it . . . and to infuse them with such power . . . to make them soar, cross the heavenly vault, to make them throw, spread over those amorphous shadows, as far as the eye can see, a closely woven scarf of a sparkling material, a path that has the brilliance, the supple hardness of steel . . . Borne by those words, along those words, dazzled, dazed, one advances . . . "The eternal silence of those infinite spaces" . . .

◈ ◈

But what's the matter with those words? What has happened to them? The sparkling scarf has become torn, frayed . . . the brilliant steel path has cracked, its debris dispersed . . .

It was as if what those words had mastered, tamed, those things to which they had communicated their splendor, their elegant austerity, suddenly, with a violent, brutal thrust, had sliced through them, dismantled them . . . and as if what had escaped . . . what is spreading . . . what is suffusing everything here . . .

But it's impossible, it's unthinkable, it doesn't exist, it can't exist . . .

Yes though, it does exist, "terrifies me," which still gets through from a great distance . . . "terrifies me" . . . a faint whimper . . . "terrifies me" . . . the trembling sound of someone else scratching, tapping . . . a fellow human being subjected to the same torture . . .

"Terrifies me" . . . the sign. The proof.

Then it's certain. That's how it is. And we've arrived. We are there. We are where there is now nothing. Nowhere. Nothing. Nothing. Nothing. Never. Nevermore. Ne-ver-more. Nothing.

◈ ◈ ◈ ◈

Arcimboldo! it's he . . . A bolide that has suddenly dropped here, God knows how, God knows where from . . . Arcimboldo whole. Arcimboldo complete. The "Arci" . . . enormous, inordinate . . . and the "bold" . . . bold, and the "o," oh so insolent, so arrogant, which raises him even higher, makes him rear up . . .

Arcimboldo. Everything here is now only his. Here, is the space he needs, to be able to take his ease, to transmit his waves as far as he wishes . . . To display his nonchalance. His effrontery.

He must bring all this and that here, everything he fancies, those flowers, those vegetables, those fruits, those incongruous objects, those strange animals, he must dispose of them in whatever way he likes . . . Arcimboldo, assurance itself. Affirmation. Challenge. Arcimboldo. Everything here is only him. Arcimboldo.